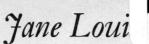
Jane Loui

THE
ICE GHOSTS
MYSTERY

A MARGARET K. MCELDERRY BOOK

AN ALADDIN BOOK
Atheneum

COPYRIGHT © 1972 BY JANE LOUISE CURRY
ALL RIGHTS RESERVED
PUBLISHED SIMULTANEOUSLY IN CANADA BY
MCCLELLAND & STEWART, LTD.
MANUFACTURED IN THE UNITED STATES OF AMERICA BY
THE MURRAY PRINTING COMPANY, FORGE VILLAGE, MASS.
ISBN 0-689-70421-6
FIRST ALADDIN EDITION

FOR COUSIN HARRIET

THE
ICE GHOSTS
MYSTERY

one

"OÖSTRUCTURE?" PERRY BIRD LIFTED ONE EARPHONE AND stared at his sister. "When did you think that one up?"

Mab lifted a hand to steady the fringe of two-inch nails that gave her mouth a formidably whiskered look. "I' a goo' 'un, i'n't it?"

"For Pete's sake, take the railroad spikes out of your mouth. It'd be just like you to swallow one when there's nobody home but me. Can you see me pedaling you all the way up to the Emergency Hospital by bicycle?" Perry stretched across the playroom cot to adjust a dial on the short-wave radio set on the bookshelf above. "Come on, what the heck is an oöstructure?"

But Mab was already off in another direction, staring up at the beamed ceiling with a rapt look on her small heart-shaped face. "You *could*, you know," she said. "Only, if I were having stomach cramps, you'd have to strap me to your sissy bar so I couldn't fall off or throw myself under the wheels of a passing Mercedes."

Perry groaned. "Can't you turn it off for five minutes? Anyhow, we'd take a nice, dull ambulance to the hospital. Now, *what*—"

With three sharp blows, Mab drove another nail. "It only means 'having to do with an egg.' Egg-shaped. Eggs are the strongest natural shape, you know. I wouldn't be surprised if oöstructures didn't turn out to be *the* shape of the future." She drove another nail, fixing a small open-ended box shape to the complicated and oddly attractive stabile sculpture growing beneath her hammer.

"Mmph. Not unless you've invented a square egg. There isn't a curved piece of wood in that whole lot." He gestured toward the large carton that held Mab's raw materials and, having lost interest, readjusted his headphones and withdrew into the shelter of a conversation between the Geophysical Observation Station in Antarctica and a ship at sea.

"Nitwit! It'll be just generally egg-shaped, like that roundish one Tigger Schultz's father paid me five dollars for. Did you know he put it in the window at the Loaf and Bottle? *This* one, I'm going to ask ten dollars for. It's going to be almost as tall as I am, and the next one I'll maybe make even bigger." Mab stepped back to survey the half-completed oöstructure with a critical eye. By squinting very hard, she could see its lines blur into the rounded bottom half of an egg. Looked at without the squint, it was a tightly packed honeycomb of pigeonhole-style boxes in odd sizes, with two—no, three—"passageways" wriggling up through the clustered shapes.

"Not bad, but . . ." Mab held one long, dark braid under her nose like a fat moustache, and thought. "It needs a bigger piece next. Too many bitty-wee cubbyholes. Now, where'd I put the saw? Perry? *Piggy!*" She hitched up her patchwork gypsy skirt and climbed over an ancient hobby horse lovingly decorated with Christmas seals, peace decals, and Wildlife Federation stamps. Shaking her brother by the shoulder, she yelled, "Perry, you lump! You're lying on my *saw*."

"Unh? What?" Perry sat up with the earphones askew. "How'd that get there?" he wondered, as Mab rolled him off the saw with a shove.

"Mmph! You'd sack out on anything, Peregrine Bird. Hold it a sec—it's snagged on your sweater." Mab freed the teeth of the saw and clambered back over the wooden horse. "There, you can go float back out over your silly kilocycles."

"A kilocycle is a unit of measurement," retorted Perry with an air of suffering patience. "I do not float out on a kilocycle. Or pedal away on one. Or . . ."

"Oh, fun*ny*."

Half an hour later both children were still so absorbed that the sound of a car and the automatic raising of the garage door below the playroom went unheard. There was a rush of footsteps on the stairs, and their older sister opened the door and looked in.

"Hi, you two. How long was the phone ringing? I heard it when I got out of the car, but it stopped before I got to the back door."

"Oh, hi, Oriole." Mab looked up from her sawing and gave a shrug. "I didn't hear it, and Perry never hears anything. Hey, are you home for the whole weekend? You could help me with this."

Oriole frowned. "Yes, I have a lot of work to do, and our dorm is *not* the place to work on a weekend. I wish I

5

knew who was phoning just now. It might've been for me. . . . Still, if it was important, whoever it was will call again." She paused. "Good grief, what *is* that thing?"

Mab explained about oöstructures while a fascinated Oriole circled the half-completed specimen and then bent down to finger the satiny wood. "You see," Mab said, "I'm going to finish it with steel wool after it's all put together, and it'll feel even groovier."

Oriole peered inside. "These things like passageways make it look like a scale model—of something like a big apartment complex. Like Habitat in Montreal. It could even be a whole community with larger units for stores and theatres. Why, Mab, it could be a *great* idea. Professor Mickleman in the Art Department over at UCLA ought to see it. Are you going to make any more of these . . . oöstructures? We ought to get you organized, make—"

"Make a *plan*."

"Yes, well, you ought. How did you come to think of it all on your own? What did—oh, now, I wonder . . ." Oriole sat down in the sawdust and looked up at her little sister with amused suspicion. "You've been reading through those old issues of *Horizon*, haven't you? I think I remember seeing an article about some architect—in New Mexico, I think it was—who designs *eco*structures? Cities of the future. Things like that. Mab?"

Mab sniffed. "Well, we artists have to take our sheer inspiration where we find it. At least the egg shape and the *oö* are mine." She squinted, tried two flat pieces of wood at right angles to each other, squeezed contact adhesive from a tube along the seam, fitted them, and secured the joint with two small nails. "It's not so nutty, you know. If an egg's about the strongest natural shape, an oö-city ought

6

to be safe from everything from sonic booms to earth-quakes."

"Mm. You'd have to ask Daddy about that," Oriole responded absently as she rose. "There goes the garage door." From the front window she said, "It's Mama and the weekend groceries. Come along down and lend a hand. Time to get organized. Perry? You, too."

The door swung gently shut, the groceries were organized into the kitchen, Molly Bird browned the chicken for the *Poulet Vallée d'Auge* she had planned for dinner, but the oblivious Perry was still afloat on the airwaves.

The Bird family lived in a comfortable fifty- or sixty-year-old frame house in Pasadena, California, where Dr. Jeffrey Bird taught seismology at the California Institute of Technology. "He's the world's next-to-greatest expert on earthquakes," Perry had explained to his class with bland assurance on his first day in first grade. At that time it was perhaps a slight—if excusable—exaggeration. Now, seven years later, Professor Bird was widely known for his uncanny capacity for absorbing reams of seismographical data from earthquake recording centers around the world—and coming up with projections on the probability of this or that disturbance in the earth's crust that were uncannily precise and often nearer the mark than computer projections.

Perry himself had once had thoughts of becoming a seismologist, but since then had settled (in succession) upon railroading, space flight, joining a Roller Derby team, deep-sea fishing, and his current passion, radio electronics. The plans for the skating career had been the shortest-lived. Too strenuous by far. There was still a lot of the old first-grade Piggy in Perry even if the baby fat had been gone for years.

At thirteen he was of medium height, stocky, with dark blond hair and blue eyes: a cheerful, comfort-loving soul, who honestly could not understand why everyone (meaning his sisters and mother) seemed always to be in a flap over something. At least once a week Mrs. Bird had occasion to cast her eyes up to the ceiling and exclaim, " 'Peregrine Comfort Bird' indeed! *Why* did we ever name you 'Comfort'? Perry, *will* you stir yourself from among the cushions and go wash your hands for dinner?"

Perry had been named "Comfort" not in anticipation of his fondness for being comfortable, but in loving reference to Mrs. Bird's own family. The Comforts—from Leicester, Massachusetts—were always doing five different things at once: one with great energy, one with unexpected efficiency, and three in a great confusion of fits and starts. Moreover, Comforts were small, dark, quick, and earnest where the Bird side of the family was fair-haired, humorous, and easy-going. Mab at eleven, small, dark, and restless, took mostly after the Comforts, Perry after the Birds. Oriole, the eldest, was caught in the middle.

Blonde, pretty Oriole was born and christened "Ariel," but after her admiring father exclaimed for the twentieth time, "She certainly is a Bird!" Molly's mischievous but deadpan answer was, "Dear me, I suppose you'll be wanting to call her 'Oriole' instead of 'Ariel.' " It had stuck. But Oriole had grown up torn between being Bird-like and Comfort-able; and the combination of a love of peace-and-things-going-smoothly with an over-supply of energy made her into an overly serious little (and then big) girl caught up in one project after another, intent on organizing her easy-going, slapdash family (and the uptight slapdash world) into a harmonious, civilized order. The Birds, the Museum

Associates, Students for Clean Sky and Seas, Winter Sports Club, the San Gabriel Free Clinic—given time she would organize them all. So far she had achieved a very limited success. Now a sophomore in elementary education at UCLA, Oriole was still saying, "What we need is a *plan,*" and the Birds were still (to her way of thinking) disorganized, unpredictable, and irresponsible.

"This does smell delicious, if I do say so myself," announced Molly Bird to her brood across the platter of fragrant chicken. "If only your father were here . . . Nothing tastes as good when he's away," she mourned, twisting the large turquoise ring on her middle finger.

"Now, no mush!" Perry sawed on an imaginary violin. "Food, that's what I want."

Mab unfolded her napkin. "*I* don't wish Daddy were here. I wish we were where *he* is." She flipped the napkin over her head, knotting it under her chin like a babushka. "Bouncing across a Swiss alp, eating brown bread and smelly goat cheese, riding in horse sleighs . . ."

"Wading around in snow up to your eyebrows," Perry offered dampingly.

"Mm, well, Oriole might meet a handsome woodcutter." Mab was not easily dampened. "I wish—"

"No!" Mrs. Bird spread her fingers wide and then touched her temples. With her eyes closed and the dark braids twisted in coils above her ears, she looked her most gypsyish. "Don't wish. The vibrations are all wrong for wishing. The stars say *eat.*"

"Mother, *please,*" Oriole moaned.

"Must you always take me seriously?" her mother peered wistfully between her fingers. "I realize that it is a great compliment to be taken seriously, but—"

Oriole shifted ground. "How *can* we eat? Where are the plates? I know you took them out of the oven."

Mrs. Bird focused on this new problem with an effort. "Plates. Well. Let's see." She tapped her chin thoughtfully with a spoon. "Do you know, I think I took them down to the basement when I went to check the pilot light on the hot water heater."

"In the middle of putting dinner on the table? Oh, Mother, *when* will you get organized?" Oriole rose with a martyred air. "The water heater! There was plenty of hot water," she could be heard complaining on the basement stairs.

"I had a feeling the pilot might have gone out, dear," Molly offered meekly.

"Had it?" Mab asked.

Her mother turned to look at her blankly. "Had what? Oh, yes, dear. I didn't tell you?" Mrs. Bird smoothed her napkin over her pretty patchwork skirt, an elegant version of Mab's own. As Oriole appeared with the plates, she flashed a disarming smile. "Thank you, dear."

The meal was delicious even if it wasn't oven-hot, for cooking was one of the five or six "things" Mrs. Bird did superbly and with every ounce of her energy and attention. She and Mab and Perry concentrated on doing justice to the chicken, potatoes *Anna,* and spinach soufflé. Oriole only picked at her food. Mrs. Bird munched and eyed her speculatively.

"If you looked a shade more soulful, Orry dear, I would suspect you'd fallen in love. Not with Harvey Trimble, I hope?"

"Yugh!" Perry grimaced expressively.

"But since you look as shocked as Perry, it must be something else."

Oriole frowned. "It's nothing, really. There was a phone call before you got home, but it stopped ringing before I got to the back door. I have this funny feeling . . . but then, it can't have been important or they'd have rung back by now, wouldn't they?"

"Why, Orry, you've had a premonition! Just like Mama," Mab exclaimed with a wicked air of innocent surprise. "How *un* practical of you."

"No such thing! I—" Oriole's breath caught as a bell shrilled once, twice, three times. "Oh, *dear*."

"S'not the phone. It's the doorbell." Perry downed his fork. "I'll get it."

Perry returned to the dinner table bearing a yellow cablegram envelope held gingerly between thumb and forefinger. Mrs. Bird had it open in a moment and smoothed the cable out with nervous fingers. She read swiftly, looking more puzzled with every word.

"It's from Daddy, in Zurich. He won't be coming home tomorrow after all." Little frown lines puckered between her eyebrows for a moment and then disappeared. "Oriole, your lost phone call must have been Western Union trying to get through to us."

"What does it *say?*" All three children spoke at once, Oriole twisting her napkin nervously, remembering her earlier uneasiness about the phone call and telling herself that premonitions were only figments of the imagination.

Mrs. Bird handed the cablegram to Oriole, who read, stared at her mother in disbelief, and passed it on. The message read:

FELICITATIONS FROM AFAR STOP IMPORTANT
WHEEDLE SKINNY INTO TAKING TEN AYEM CLASS
ALSO RESEARCH STUDENTS STOP AM GOING SKIING
WITH GUS BACHNER STOP HOME ON THE THIRD.

LOVE

JEFF

Perry and Mab groaned in unison, "It's not *fair!*"

"Daddy cutting classes?" said Oriole. "I don't believe it. Not to go *skiing.*"

"Your father always has his reasons." Molly Bird answered distantly, absentmindedly stirring what was left of the spinach soufflé into a green soup. "But you're right. It isn't at all like Jeffrey. I'm afraid Skinny is going to think it very peculiar."

"Who's Gus Bachner?" Perry asked.

"Who? Oh, Gus Bachner. He was—*is* a geologist. A friend of your father's from graduate school days."

"Oh well, then." Oriole brightened. "It doesn't have to look as if Daddy's exactly playing hooky. Couldn't you tell Professor Esterbrook it's something to do with the Earth Sciences Conference? 'Further investigations in the field'?"

Mrs. Bird shook her head firmly, the golden hoops of her earrings swinging. "I will not fib to Skinny, Oriole. If your father is skiing, there has to be a perfectly good and urgent reason." The little frown of worry returned. "I do hope he bought some good waterproof gloves and something for over his ears."

Oriole gave a wistful sigh, her disapproval forgotten. "I wish *I* were off skiing in Switzerland." Mab and Perry nodded in glum agreement.

"Sorry, old dears. You'll just have to make do with a

piece of chocolate cake," their mother announced briskly, getting up to remove the dinner plates and bring on the dessert. But the little frown of concern remained. Professor Bird had neglected—on purpose?—to say where he was off to. The Earth Sciences Conference had been held in Zurich. So the nearest skiing would be at . . .

Several minutes later, Mab and Oriole found Molly in the living room poring over the world atlas, the forgotten chocolate cake spinning slowly to a stop on the hi-fi turntable.

The third of February came and went with no Professor Bird. Not only no Professor Bird in Pasadena, but no Professor Bird anywhere Professor Bird could or should have been. At seven o'clock on the morning of the sixth the persistent ringing of the telephone awakened the worried family to a sadly garbled but nonetheless frightening cablegram message from Professor Augustus Bachner in Salzburg, in Austria:

KRANKENSCHWESTER SENDS FOR ME THIS STOP DO
NOT COMMA REPEAT DO NOT BELIEVE AVALANCHE
STORY STOP IT WAS TCE GHOSTS STOP IT WAS STOP
STOP

BACHNER

"*Austria?*"

"Avalanche story? What avalanche story?"

"Who's Krankenschwester?"

Mrs. Bird broke into the confusion of questions. "*Krankenschwester* means 'nurse' in German. Now, hush!"

Putting their heads together, the Birds still could not make head or tail of the strange message. "TCE"—the Western Union operator insisted it read "TCE"—must be an error for

13

"THE." "GHOSTS" made no sense at all, and the word "AVA-
LANCHE" made them extremely nervous. However, they
did not have much time to puzzle over it. At eight o'clock
the telephone rang. Mrs. Bird's alarm was echoed in the
children's faces when she covered the mouthpiece to whisper, "Washington! The *State Department*." She listened,
pale and very quiet and looking very young, nodding every
now and then and saying, "Yes, I understand, but . . ."

Hanging up at last, she turned an unbelieving look upon
the children. "They say—they say your father w-was lost
in an avalanche, and that Dr. Bachner is in the hospital with
severe head injuries. But . . ." Drawing herself up to her
full five-feet-two, eyes narrowed fiercely, she looked as if
she might be seeing all the way to Austria. "But *I do not
believe it*. Perry, you're dressed; go out and get the paper.
Oriole, stop sniffling and set the table for breakfast. And
you, Mab, can just waltz upstairs and put on your slippers."

The Sunday *Los Angeles Times*, when Perry had fetched
it in from the front porch, started Oriole off again. The
banner headline read: NOTED CALTECH SCIENTIST SWALLOWED
BY GLACIER. Oriole sobbed; Mab and Perry were stunned
to see the awful news in print so soon; but Mrs. Bird's eyes
narrowed again. Purposefully, this time. Marching into the
kitchen, she put on her old paint and dye-stained work
apron and took eggs and bacon out of the refrigerator.

"Lock the front door, Perry," she called. "When Mab
comes down, have her close the front drapes. There will be
reporters. We are not going to be At Home. We haven't
any answers for ourselves, let alone for the newspapers.
First it was an avalanche, and now it's a crevasse in a glacier,
but Gus Bachner said something about ghosts, and he must
have meant *some*thing by it."

The children appeared in the doorway as if by magic. Molly turned to find all three eyeing her suspiciously, but took no notice. She waved the egg whisk. "After breakfast get out your suitcases and snow things. Ski boots, plenty of warm sweaters, and your long woollies. Not the skis. We'll rent skis when we get there." She broke another egg into the bowl and promptly sat down on a nearby chair with the eggshell still in her hand. Reaching into the apron pocket with the other hand, she drew out a felt pen and jotted *Absolutely Necessary Gear* on a corner of her apron and below it a list beginning with *German dictionary, 1st aid kit, J's field glasses.*

"When we get *where?*" wailed Oriole between sniffles. "How *can* you all be so hard-hearted?" Perry had already headed for the storeroom and the suitcases, and Mab could be heard in the hall calmly dialing the vet to arrange for the boarding-out of Phyllis, the Birds' large and shaggy English sheep dog.

"Where?" Mrs. Bird answered Oriole vaguely. "I'm not perfectly sure, dear. Here, take this. You don't mind finishing the omelet, do you? I think I will go upstairs and think." She handed over the beaten eggs in their copper bowl and drifted past Mab into the hall and up the stairs. On the landing she paused to add to the list on her apron a cryptic note: *All tht nyl. rope.*

"Oh, dear!" Oriole wiped away her tears and turned a stricken look on Mab, who was having no luck raising anyone at the vet's. "Mabbit, if she's going to ask that ouija board, I'll *die*. There must be *some*thing sensible we can do. If she means we're going to try to find out what's happened to Daddy, we'll have to get *organized*. We—"

"—need a *plan*," sighed Mab.

two

"MAMA SAID THE EXTRA GERMAN PHRASE BOOK WAS IN HERE,
but I can't find it," Mab sighed. "Suntan lotion. Airmail
stamps . . ." Opening the second compartment of her
mother's suitcase, she let out a whoop. The old, worn
ouija board lay atop the neatly folded stacks of sweaters,
socks, and warm tights. "Poor Oriole!" She giggled.

Perry hopped in from the smaller bedroom of their Salzburg hotel suite, to all appearances trying to tie a shoelace
as he hopped. "Why 'Poor Oriole'? Uh, I see." He sat on
the edge of a chair to undo and retie the lace. "What I
don't see is why the heck that thing bugs Orry so. Sure,
it's nutty. But it isn't as if Mom really believed in that mor-
bid spirit junk."

Mab shrugged. "Who knows? I suppose if it wasn't the
ouija it'd be something else. Orry would be purely flap-
stracted if she didn't have something to moan over." Mab
rooted under the sweaters, but found only a manila folder
full of newspaper clippings fastened together with a plastic

16

clothespin. "It used to spook me a little too," she confided. "Mama's holding conferences with a piece of painted wood, I mean. So I just asked her about it. She said Orry was being a silly goose and that all she used it for was a sort of Aid to Concentration, a game she plays with herself to get her thoughts unjumbled. You let your subconscience come through your fingers to move the planchette. Or something like that."

"Subconscious," Perry corrected. "That's all the stuff you've got in your head that you don't pay any attention to. I think. It still sounds pretty far out. Maybe you'd better put the board under the clothes so Oriole won't go all martyred on us if she's around when Mom opens the thing up again. It's bad enough her weeping like a waterworks every time anyone mentions Pop." Perry pulled on his heavy windbreaker and looked around for his gloves. His own voice wavered a little over the name.

"Piggy? Do you really and truly believe Daddy's alive, like Mama says?" Mab looked up from the suitcase, her eyes suspiciously shiny. "And that we're going to find him?"

Perry frowned. The way Mab went on about being an artist, or about the latest nutty fairy tale she was writing, Perry tended to forget that she wasn't as grown-up as she pretended. "Sure," he said gruffly, feeling not at all sure. "Isn't Mom always right about that sort of thing? Like knowing what Pop's thinking, I mean, and if he's going to be late to dinner, and all?"

Mab brightened. "I hadn't thought of that. The way she feels about Daddy, she'd just *know*. There's nobody in the world with a better woman's institution than Mama."

Perry looked blank for a moment, then exclaimed, "There you go again. Woman's *intuition*, chucklehead. Come on,

17

get your coat on. You'd better come with me. We can pick up a couple of phrase books at that shop just across the Staatsbrucke, that bridge down the street. Then I have to find someplace where we can buy . . ." He fished in a jacket pocket to bring out a list written in Mrs. Bird's squiggly hand. "Let's see: two more flashlights, four pairs of snow goggles, some snack stuff, and some extra batteries."

"Rots of ruck." Mab pulled on her old woolly Scots tam. "What do you bet the phrase books don't have a word for 'goggles'?"

Perry sighed. "I'll use sign language. Look, idiot infant, if you're coming, put on your boots and *come*."

"Boots?" Mab looked at her stockinged feet thoughtfully. "Ah, boots."

The Birds had flown, by way of New York and Brussels, to Salzburg. They had been a little delayed, as it had taken until late on Monday to find accommodations for Phyllis, whose heart-broken "why-have-they-abandoned-me?" howl was notorious in the Pasadena kennel world. *Canis non gratus*, Professor Bird had once quipped. Finally, thanks to the innocence of the receptionist at the Bide-a-Night Pet Hotel, the Birds made the Tuesday morning flight to New York.

Arriving in Salzburg on Wednesday the ninth, Mrs. Bird and the children took a taxi directly from the airport to the Landkrankenhaus, a modest hospital in the Mülln district—only to find Dr. Bachner gone. "Totally collapsed in the mind, you understand, no? We do not here have the facilities for such, therefore the Herr Doktor yesterday has been removed to Vienna, to the Sigmundhaus, which has for such ailments a specialty," the doctor who had treated Bachner

18

explained with much waving of hands. "All the time he was—how you say?—raving. About impossibilities. The tragedy of his friend was for him too much, *nicht wahr?* Most regrettable, dear Madame. You would wish to have the direction of the Sigmundhaus, *nein?*"

Mrs. Bird wished to have the address, yes; but on the other hand, it would not do to waste time traveling to Vienna to visit a Gus Bachner who was totally collapsed in the mind. A telephone call to the American Embassy in Vienna brought an answering call from the Embassy's Consular Section the next morning. Professor Bachner was still incoherent; and though his physical condition was no longer critical, the Sigmundhaus did not allow him to have visitors. No, the Embassy did not know where Professors Bird and Bachner had been staying. Nor where the accident had taken place. Bachner had been found on the Tricklfall trail above Abtenau, but there was no telling how far he might have come.

Oriole's pleas that the family make a dignified retreat home to California were firmly overruled. To Mab's and Perry's questions about where they *were* going, Mrs. Bird gave evasive answers. She disappeared for two hours after lunch, returning to the hotel to closet herself with Baedeker's *Tyrol and Salzburg* guide book, an armload of other guide books and maps, Wednesday's Paris edition of the *New York Herald-Tribune* and, Mab suspected, the ouija board.

An hour later she reappeared in the hotel coffee shop to announce, "Riesenmoos. That's where we're going. Riesenmoos. You'll have to pack tonight. We have to get up very early to catch the first train."

Oriole, who had spent the early afternoon eating chocolate cake and drinking coffee in the Glockenspiel Cafe in the company of a mournful and wonderfully sympathetic young man she had met in the American Express office, looked dismayed. She had obviously abandoned all thought of a dignified retreat to Pasadena and become reconciled to a stay in Salzburg.

"Riesenmoos? Where's that?" asked Mab.

"Why Riesenmoos?" Perry put in shrewdly. "You've heard something about Pop!"

"No, dears. I wish I had. No. But I've been thinking about something your father said several weeks ago—something about a puzzle he wished he had time to look into. He never said exactly what it was, you see: only that it was very curious—'a very unnatural disturbance pattern.' I think it had something to do with this very unpredictable winter Europe is having and all those spotty little earthquakes in places with odd names like Ptuj and Stupnik. Daddy left behind a lot of newspaper clippings about that sort of thing, but I can't make head or tail of them. I should have asked Skinny, I suppose, but one always thinks of such things too late, and you know I never can keep anything about tremor patterns and the Richter scale straight in my head for five minutes."

"Then why Riesenmoos?" asked Oriole plaintively.

"Because *this* was in the folder with the clippings." Mrs. Bird produced a Shell road map of Austria and spread it out on the table, moving napkins, silver, and empty cups aside. "There." She pointed.

In the middle of the map, an inch and a quarter southeast of Salzburg, the mountainous district marked "Tennen-Geb." was lightly shaded in with Dr. Bird's familiar blue pencil. The district was circled by roads indicated as highways or main roads, running from Golling, south of Salzburg, to Werfen, Pfarr-Werfen, Huttau, St. Martin, Annaberg, Abtenau, and back to Golling. A secondary road running up into the high valleys south of the highest peaks connected Pfarr-Werfen with Werfenweng and the even more remote Riesenmoos. Mab, peering closely, wondered whether the faint circular scratches on the shaded portion that converged on Riesenmoos' tiny dot were her father's doing or the ouija's planchette's.

"Abtenau." Perry looked up. "Isn't that near where Dr. Bachner was found?"

"Yes." Molly nodded. "*But.* Think, now: if you were interested in those mountains, would you have stayed in Abtenau?" She tapped the map.

"No-o," Perry said slowly. "I guess I'd want to get as high up as I could."

Producing the fat red Baedeker guide from her handbag, Mrs. Bird opened it to a more detailed map of the Tennen-Gebirge. "The highest and the closest to the center of the range is this little valley . . . here. The Eiswinkel."

"And Riesenmoos is up in the Eiswinkel," Oriole finished for her. "Oh, it's all very logical, I'm sure, Mama, but . . ." The objection trailed off. Arguing was useless when Mrs. Bird wore her Sweetly Faraway look. And she had it now. "I think I'll go out for a cup of coffee." Oriole sighed.

"But you've coffee right here . . . Oh, but that child can be tiresome!" Mrs. Bird remarked under her breath as the coffee-shop door swung shut after Oriole. "Let's see, now. I've already phoned for hotel reservations, but I forgot to arrange to have the *Herald-Tribune* sent up. It won't do to get out of touch with the rest of the world. I'll see to that next, and the train tickets." She rose and pulled on the

21

long coat that with her knee-high boots made her look like an oddly tiny Cossack. "Perry dear, would you mind picking up one or two little things for me? If you think you'll need the German phrase book to get along in the shops, it's upstairs in my large suitcase." She fished a crumpled list from her pocket, tucked it in his hand, drank off Oriole's abandoned coffee, wrapped Oriole's untouched piece of hazelnut cake in a paper napkin, putting it in her pocket, and hurried out, looking efficient.

Riesenmoos, according to the guide books, was a small farming village, fifty-seven kilometers from Salzburg, Elevation: 4832 ft.; Population: 225. The Eiswinkel was described as a "sleepy little valley time seems to have forgotten, nestled in its little niche in the great wall of steep, rounded limestone peaks ringing the rugged Tennen-Gebirge plateau between the impressive Königskogel peak and the no less stately Kreuzkogel." What the guide-book clichés gave no hint of was the wild loveliness of the Salzach Valley in a snow shower as the train wound upward out of Salzburg and through the Lueg Pass. Outside the old market town of Werfen, the great castle of Höhenwerfen crowned a high wooded hill set against a towering backdrop of mountains. A vision out of a fairy tale, it silenced even Mab, who had been kept busy exclaiming "O-o!" and "Look there!" as she switched from the window side of the train compartment to the window in the corridor.

Perry was more struck by a sign glimpsed near the Werfen station, indicating the route to a place called the "Eisriesenwelt." In smaller print—in English, apparently for the benefit of tourists—it read, "World's Largest Ice Cave."

Perry leaned forward. "Hey, Mom? What does 'Eisriesenwelt' mean? And 'Geschlossen Oktober-Maï'—is that 'Closed from October to May'?"

"Yes, that's right. 'Eisriesenwelt'? My guess would be 'The Ice Giants' World.' But that doesn't make sense, does it? Perhaps it's some legend to do with the caverns. There seem to be quite a few caves in these limestone mountains. We'll have to look that one up in the book when we unpack," she added with a thoughtful squint before taking up her *Herald-Tribune* again. "Have you seen? There's been another earthquake. In Zagreb this time."

"Too bad it's closed." Perry's mind was still on the caves. "Places like that are really cool. I wonder what it would be like to be a speleologist and go exploring caves all over the world? Pretty neat, I'll bet."

"What's an ice cave?" asked Mab. "A cave in a glacier?"

Perry explained with the heavy brotherly kindness that could be counted on to make Mab writhe. "Of *course* not. It's a regular cave, where the limestone's been worn away by water. You know about that, don't you? Well, the ice kind is all a matter of ventilation. In early summer the cold air from deep down in gets swept up and out, so that it freezes the water that seeps into the caves when the snow melts. Then in winter the cold air blows *in. Verstehen Sie?*"

"Oh, yes. I understand." Mab patted a small yawn elegantly, then ducked quickly, cowering down in her corner as Perry flashed out a hand to give her arm a fox-bite pinch. "No, not that! Anything but that!" she pleaded in a dramatic, whispery shriek.

"Mavis Bird!" Oriole stiffened and sent her a wounded look. "*Please!* You are not, in case you don't remember, on your way to a fun fair. This is a serious—a serious investigative expedition." To Byron Fleischacker, the young man who sat next to the compartment door in the seat opposite her, she murmured apologetically, "The young forget easily."

Mab and Perry, reminded of their father, subsided guiltily, but could not resist rolling their eyes at each other over Oriole's martyred tone. Even Molly Bird's attention twitched away from her Yugoslavian earthquake, but she hid her smile behind the paper. Oriole had, since her discovery of Byron Fleischacker in the American Express office, left off weeping and taken up Looking Brave. Austria was not only the place to be, but the discovery of Professor Bird's fate was a Sacred Duty. Byron was—"Isn't it a small world?" Oriole had breathed—a UCLA graduate student doing research for a study of "Superstitious Survivals in Isolated Mountain Communities," and the isolated mountain community he was headed for happened to be Riesenmoos. That and the fact that he was not only Serious and Responsible but looked at her with adoring cocker spaniel eyes decided Oriole. It was clearly her duty to see that the Birds left no stone in Riesenmoos unturned in their sad search.

"Er—um, ah, Peregrine?" Byron cleared his throat apologetically. "About those caves. You might be interested in some of the stories I've run across in my researches. All superstition, of course, but fascinating. Once upon a time— up until not so very many years ago, in fact, there were strange tales around this part of the country about huge columns of cave ice coming to life." Byron's enthusiasm for his subject seemed to bring him to life, too. His voice dropped dramatically. "Great slab-footed, icicle-fingered giants with windy voices, who retreated deep into the mountain as the summer deepened."

"Man!" Perry stared. "People really thought they saw them?"

Byron recovered his serious, scholarly tone and, with a self-conscious smile, said, "Well, yes and no. At bottom it's an explanation of the yearly return of the ice. There are a lot of winter myths—the retreat of Old Man Winter, the defeat of the Winter King by summer's champion—and the giants are a nice variation." He mused. "It's just my luck that nobody believes in such things any more. Oh, there are a lot of superstitions floating around, but very few real 'survivals.' People keep the old legends on more as tourist attractions than anything else. At Carnival in Imst, there are more strangers on hand than townspeople, all come to watch the *Schemenlaufen* procession. A 'quaint custom.' What a lot of people don't realize is that their quaint customs have their roots in a time when the *Schemen* were the demons of winter, and the rituals—long before they degenerated into 'performances' and then parades— the rituals *had* to finish with their being chased out of town, or springtime *couldn't* have come." He sat back, a bit embarrassed. "Sorry to bore you with a lecture on the subject. But they are nice little myths."

Oriole stifled a yawn and watched the mountains unroll past the corridor window, but Perry and Mab were fascinated. "*Sch—Schemen?* What does it mean?" asked Mab.

Byron considered. "I suppose that *Schemenlaufen* means —literally—'the running of the shadows.' But *Schemen* in such legends almost always means 'ghosts'."

four hundred and ninety-nine years, Riesenmoos played *Der Eisschemenlaufen* again. He doesn't believe it can be authentic. But if it *were* true that somehow they have preserved a book of the old play, and if they were to perform it again this year, I could tape the entire celebration. It would be a . . . a real find," he finished shyly.

Mab craned forward to see her mother's reaction. "Mama! *Eisschemen*—wouldn't that be . . . ?"

"The Ice Ghosts." Perry finished for her. "That 'TCE' in Dr. Bachner's cable? It was a mistake for 'ICE,' not for 'THE'!"

To the younger children's delight, Mrs. Bird calmly folded her hands in her lap and, with a quirk of one eyebrow in Oriole's direction, smiled sweetly. "Yes, Byron, that *is* very interesting. We may be in Riesenmoos long enough to see your play. It would be on Shrove Tuesday, wouldn't it? Next Tuesday?" At his nod, she gave Oriole an innocent smile and said pointedly, "I'm surprised that Oriole hasn't ferreted out more about your work, Byron. I'm sure she will be most interested in hearing everything you learn about your 'Ice Ghosts,' won't you, Orry dear?"

"Yes, Mother," Oriole said meekly. Privately, she thought it distinctly unfair that her mother's hunches, with or without the aid of a ouija board, should so invariably be right. Riesenmoos. Well. It would be a comfort if only her mother could be right about Professor Bird's being alive— and wrong about *some*thing.

For the rest of the journey Oriole half listened to Byron's earnest account of a survival of snake worship in the mountains of West Virginia. Mab and Perry watched another slowly gathering snowstorm break at last, hiding the further trees and mountain slopes, while Mrs. Bird dozed off as if she hadn't a care in the world. The post-bus swayed on, stopping now and then to pick up or discharge passengers, parcels, and mail. A small group of young people in skiing gear disembarked at Werfenweng and retrieved their skis from the rack on the tail end of the bus. The winding climb up into the Eiswinkel saw the Birds and Byron alone in the bus except for the driver and a wizened old man in a broad-brimmed hat, who regarded them with suspicion. Perry, suffering the first twinges of a toothache, glared right back.

In Riesenmoos it seemed that Mrs. Bird could not only be wrong about something, but that she had managed to get her little brood awkwardly stranded. "But no, Madame," said the clerk at the little Hotel Gappenwirt. "There is no reservation in the name of Bird. You have made a mistake, no? It is most regrettable. No, Madame, we have the gross misfortune to have no rooms free at all, not one." Byron, who was booked into the Hotel Post, swept them along with him. But the owner of the even smaller Hotel Post, with its richly carved balconies and grotesque grinning faces on the door lintel, looked Molly up and down, taking in her stylish Cossack coat and wine-colored boots, and said, "It is indeed a pity, Frau Bird, that you come when all of the rooms which are not booked are being repainted. A great pity. Perhaps the Pension Mooserkreuz?" But Frau Nohl of the Pension Mooserkreuz edged the Birds toward her door, smiling all the while, as she repeated, "Sorry, no room free. No room free. *Verstehen Sie? Nicht zimmer frei.*"

"*Ja, ich verstehe.* I certainly do understand," answered Molly Bird with a little nod. Her politely wooden expression lasted only until they were once more in the snowy street. "So Riesenmoos doesn't want to have anything to do with the Birds," she said grimly. "Very interesting. You can't tell me there aren't rooms going a-begging in this village. There's hardly a soul to be seen in the streets."

"It is odd," Oriole admitted reluctantly. Pointing back the way they had come, she indicated a snug little hut at the upper corner of the sloping, snowy field below the road. "The sign says *Ski Schule*, and there's someone— the ski instructor, I guess—inside, but you can tell from the snow that there haven't been any skiers on that field, at least not since the last really big snow."

Perry rolled a snowball and held it against his aching jaw. He frowned, stamping his feet to stir up the circulation. "It's good snow, too. You'd think a place as cool as this would be overrun. It's not *that* hard to get to."

Mab tugged her mohair scarf up around her mouth and squinted her eyes, achieving an expression she hoped was enigmatic. "Zair ees—'ow you say?—bad feelink in zis place. Ze air, she is throbbink wiz mistrustings, no?"

"Ze air, she is throbbink wiz mistrustings, yes," said Oriole with a thoughtful squint of her own. As she usually greeted Mab's accents and poses with a brief lecture entitled "Be Yourself," this unexpected sally was received with some surprise.

"Well, yes," said Molly, turning a brief flicker of interest on her elder daughter before striking on up the snowy road toward the last of the board-and-room *pensions*, perched high above the village at the bottom of the steep field called the Riesenalm. "The fact that we're obviously not wanted," she panted, "—even if there weren't other reasons—makes me *sure* we've come right. People acting so afraid, not wanting to have anything to do with us—it

30

must have something to do with Jeffrey."

"We should've called ourselves 'Vogel' and come in disguise," said Mab, darkly.

Perry snorted. "As if they wouldn't know that 'Bird' is the English for 'Vogel.' They do speak some English, featherhead. Some of them, anyway."

"Well, 'Oiseau' then. Or 'Avis'." The words and Mab's breath frosted out in ragged little clouds through the mohair scarf. She struggled up the steep road at the tail of the procession, her suitcase bumping against her knee at every step.

"Mavis Avis!" Perry mocked, ploughing after the unusually silent Oriole.

The wooden house at the foot of the Riesenalm had more the look of the Tyrol, to the west, than of Salzburg Province. A balcony ran around the front half of the upper story, and the low-pitched roof was decorated with a little belfry and weighted with blocks of stone. But if Haus Strumpf, as the carving on the heavy door named it, was more rustic and had fat, cheerful angels carved above the door instead of gargoyles, its windows were as dark and uninviting as any in the village below. The stillness of the rapidly dying afternoon was broken only by the occasional mournful bleat of goats and the moo of a cow. The woods above were dark, the air dank and heavy. The Birds looked at each other doubtfully.

"This can't be a *pension*," Oriole protested. "The back end of the house is a barn!"

"It's listed as a *pension* with full board in the guide book, and at this point I am not going to object to good, clean animal smells," was Mrs. Bird's firm answer. "Even if we could catch a ride down to Werfenweng, we've probably missed the last bus out to Pfarr-Werfen." Taking hold of the string of sleigh bells that hung by the side of the door-post, she gave them a determined jangle. The children held their breath as if they half expected something unspeakable to answer the door.

For a long while there was no answer at all. Then a small face appeared briefly at a window, and small scuffling noises moved toward the door. The sound of three heavy bolts being drawn back made even Mrs. Bird blink. What were the Strumpfs barring out? She managed resolutely to ignore Oriole's hand pulling at her sleeve. The small scuffling noise turned out to be a small, blond boy in an oversize pair of sealskin slipper-boots. His wrists and neck were painfully thin, and bright, dark eyes gave him a nervous, birdlike look.

"Er—*Grüss Gott,*" said Mrs. Bird in polite greeting.

"*Grüss Gott. Was wollen Sie?*" The question was almost a whisper.

"Do you have—um, no, that won't do. *Haben Sie ein Zimmer frei? Wir sind vier Personen.*"

"English? American?" The small boy produced a large grin. "I have English. I have learned in school now four years, and by the wireless before it goed in the autumn. And I practice with my friend Gabriel, who has worked in England one year. Pretty good, no?" Casting a doubtful look over his shoulder, he hesitated, then opened the door wide. Beckoning the Birds in, he said in a rush, "We have two good rooms for fifty schillings together. Two beds there are in each, O.K.? So, good. But I forget my manners." He bowed formally. "I am Hansl Strumpf, having twelve years of age, the son of Kani Strumpf, the woodcutter, and Elisabeth, the best baker of *Kugelhupf* in the whole of the

Eiswinkel, who is presently feeding the cow, I think."

"Charmed, I'm sure," said Mrs. Bird, answering his bow with a graceful curtsey that made him laugh and Oriole wince.

Perry's slumbering appetite stirred at the word "baker." "What's *Kugelhupf?*"

Kugelhupf, as the Birds shortly discovered, was a delicious crumbly cake baked in a deep ring mold with a swirling pattern. They also discovered themselves, coats spirited away, seated in the warm kitchen around a pine table scrubbed almost white, eating *Kugelhupf* and drinking steaming *Mokka* coffee. Hansl puttered around the gleaming wood-burning stove, boiling more water and grinding more coffee and keeping up a steady stream of questions in a mixture of German and English about spacemen, American food, Perry's favorite rock group, and whether this Creedence Clearwater was a person or the whole group.

"*Hansl! Wer sind diese. . . . Warum sind sie in meiner Küche?*"

The shrill question startled everyone. A thin, haggard woman carrying an almost-empty milk pail closed the door that apparently gave onto the stable and dairy end of the house, stared at the group around the table, and repeated in German, "Hansl, who are these people? Why are they in my kitchen?"

"It is all right, Mama. I have rented the guest rooms. For fifty schillings. Was that right?"

Elisabeth Strumpf put a nervous hand to her brow. "I—I do not know. To have strangers in the house now . . . *Ach*, yes, you meant well, *Liebling*. Fifty schillings is good." She lifted the pail onto a small work table, wiped her hands on the flowered apron that covered her dirndl skirt, and smoothed a stray wisp of faded blonde hair into place under her coronet of braids. To Mrs. Bird she said, "It is long since we have guests. You forgive me, *bitte*."

"Not at all, Frau Strumpf." Mrs. Bird rose and reached over to shake her hand, saying slowly in her rusty German, "I am Molly Bird, and these are my children. Oriole, Mab, and Perry. Your Hansl has made us so much at home that I forgot we had not introduced ourselves. You are saving our lives, you know. We were beginning to think we might have to spend a cold night in the church."

"B-Bird?" Frau Strumpf paled. "You are Frau Bird? *Gott in Himmel!* You must not stay here. My husband . . . I must find my husband. He is late for his coffee." Twisting her apron strings around her fingers, she edged toward the dairy door and disappeared through it with the nervous scuttle of a frightened hen.

Hansl looked for a moment as if he might follow, but he swallowed nervously and stayed. Somewhere at the back of his pale blue eyes was a gleam of excitement as he said to the bewildered Birds, "Please not to worry. My father will make it all right, you will see. It is difficult to explain. I am not to speak of it, you understand, but Mama has been unlike herself since ten days. Last night even she burned the schnitzels."

"Ten days ago?" The Birds exchanged glances.

"*Ja.*" Hansl nodded. "When she has seen the ghost."

four

"Where can Hansl be? He said he'd meet us here as soon as his school was out for lunch." Mab peered into the village street through a window display of knit scarves and caps, hand-carved wooden figurines, tinned sausages, and miniature bottles of Eiswinkel apple brandy. The *Lebensmittel Metzger* sold everything Riesenmoos could possibly need; and if Mab saw no Hansl coming along the Moosweg, she did see a red tasseled hood too pretty to resist trying on.

Frau Metzger, behind the dairy counter helping a thin, stooped gentleman with a large order for eggs, bacon, milk, and butter, began to look a bit more cheerful. The little girl looked very fetching in the knitted hood. Clearly it meant a sale, and if Frau Metzger was wary of strangers, she was not in the least wary of their money. "*Ach, sehr schön, kleine Fräulein!* Very pretty, and thirty schillings only."

Perry looked up from his boot-lacing with a pained expression. "If Hansl isn't here by the time I get these spaghetti-straps tied, I'm not going to wait. I'm starved. That soup we had was good, but I think what this tooth-ache and I need is a big piece of cake, some hot chocolate, and a couple of aspirin."

"Not me. I'm stuffed." Mab clumped over to the dry-goods counter in her newly fitted ski boots, fished her change purse from the depths of a ski-trouser pocket, and counted out thirty schillings. "Just don't you go off with-out paying the rent for the skis and boots. I haven't got enough. There. *Dreissig schillings, ja?*"

Frau Metzger swept the coins from the counter, all the while keeping an eye on her other customer, who was now hovering over the first-aid supplies. *"Dreissig, ja. Danke schön.* And how long the skis for, please? Two days? Three?"

"It all depends," said Perry glumly, as he pulled out his wallet. Molly had cautioned against their volunteering any information until they knew better what ailed Riesenmoos. "Can I give you for today now, and more tomorrow if we stay over?"

"Ja, ja. Sehr gut. Very good. I write down the numbers of the skis, so. You stay at Haus Strumpf, *nicht wahr?*"

"That's right."

Perry, absorbed in smoothing out a crumpled hundred schilling note, had his back to Frau Metzger's gentleman customer, whom the mention of the Strumpf house startled out of a deep contemplation of elastic bandages. Mab, tying the tasseled cord of her new hood, saw and supposed it was only curiosity. Perhaps he knew Kani and Elisabeth Strumpf. But when Frau Metzger spelled out "P. B-i-r-d" aloud as she entered it in the rental book, Mab turned quickly so that the man would not see her watching him. It

36

was silly, of course, but she had the distinct impression that he had . . . *unfolded* at the sound of "Bird," rather like an accordion pleat being ironed out smooth. By the time she could sneak another look, he had folded himself back into his accustomed stoop. With bristly dark hair, a thin beak of a nose, and a long neck that stuck out instead of up, he looked remarkably like Arthur Rackham's drawing of a talkative elderberry tree in her mother's old copy of *Peter Pan in Kensington Gardens*. Well, a *little* like. More like an amiable crested buzzard. If there was such a thing.

About the "amiable" she began to be less sure. The man smiled and nodded appreciatively over his purchases as Frau Metzger added them up, and gave a two-schilling tip to a small Metzger for carrying his boxes to the Karmann-Ghia parked in front of the store; but as he folded himself down into the driver's seat, Mab, safe inside the shop, had the oddest sense that he was fuming with anger. Trembling, wordless anger that almost made the air crackle. It made not a bit of sense, Mab knew, but the feeling was almost palpable. "I wonder if that's what Mama calls an 'aura'?" she thought. "He almost turns the air red." Then, with a roar, he was gone.

"I don't think I like that man," Mab announced to no one in particular.

"Who?" said Perry, observant as ever. He pulled on his mittens. "What man?"

"*Doktor Pfnür?*" Frau Metzger was shocked into a stream of thickly accented English. "*Ach*, Herr Doktor Pfnür is of men the kindest, the most admired. You must not speak such things. So much he gives to Riesenmoos—the new images of Saint George and Saint Martin in the church, the repairings of the organ, the Friday night films in the village hall, the new ski-lift—all these things. Not so much now as before, perhaps. His school does not go so good, and he worries much, I think. It may be the ski lift runs very little because we now have so few visitors, but Riesenmoos remembers how large is the heart of Herr Doktor Pfnür."

Perry, embarrassed, gave Mab a furious glare, gathered up his skis, and stumped out of the shop. Mab managed an apologetic mumble and a timid smile, tugged on her gloves, and with a hasty *"Wiedersehen"* followed Perry's example.

But she did not follow Perry. Shouldering her skis, she dawdled along the Moosweg, looking in its three or four shop windows, gradually making her way in the direction of the neat stucco schoolhouse. Halfway there she saw Hansl running to meet her, his bright orange scarf flying. He slowed as he came up, panting a little, his breath frosting out in clouds.

"I am sorry to be late." He swallowed, caught his breath, and plunged on. "Fräulein Muhlbach kept me in for not paying attention. I was thinking, you see, of what you asked: that we should find what my schoolmates know of Herr Professor Bird, your father, and the Ice Ghosts. I was thinking how it will be exciting, this detection. Then Teacher asks me what is the capital of Upper Volta, and I do not hear her. So! Now there is no time to—how do you say?—to 'pump' my friends." He slid a sidelong look toward Mab as if to see how she took this delay. "But there is time yet for me to make you known to my friend Gabriel, who is teacher of the ski school. Where is your brother, Perry Green?"

Mab giggled. "Peregrine. But just 'Perry' is better. He's at the sweet shop, the *Konditorei*." She swung around, narrowly missing a plate glass window with her skis. "Actually," she explained, "we can pump your friends any time. It's just that Oriole thought we ought to have a plan, so Mama decided we all had to set out with our little phrase books. Byron Fleischacker—he's a friend of my sister's— Byron has to interview all of the old folks anyway, because he collects legends from mountain people for his work. So that leaves the younger women to Mama, the men to Oriole, and the kids to Perry and me. Only, Oriole doesn't speak *any* German, and she gets flustered having to look things up in a phrase book or dictionary all the time. Like this morning, when she was practicing 'Have you ever seen an Ice Ghost?' and it came out 'Have you sat down on an Ice Ghost yet?' "

Hansl gave a yelp of delight and, taking a running start, skated halfway up the path to the door of the *Konditorei*. "Ho, I like that! I wish she will ask that of my friend Gabriel, who very much likes pretty girls. He will say only '*Noch nicht*'—not yet. For he, too, wishes very much to see the ghosts, but he also is a foreigner, from the Tyrol. I tell him if he sees one he will soon be dead, like in the old tales. You see . . . *Ach*, I am sorry again!" Seeing Mab's stricken look, he broke off, catching at her arm as she reached to open the shop door. "It is only what the old folk say, you understand. I do not believe it. Such things—"

Mab's chin went up. Looking Hansl in the eye, she said, "I know it isn't true. Professor Bachner was with Daddy, and *he* saw them—and he's not dead. Only funny in the head," she added unhappily.

"There, you see?" Hansl spoke earnestly. "Perhaps your Papa, too, ran from them. Perhaps he has fallen on his head and lost his remembering. He could be in any place. Annaberg or Abtenau. In America, even. It is certain he is not in Riesenmoos. This 'plan' you have: it is a waste of time. All your questions will not find him here."

"You sound like everyone else," Mab said sullenly. "I thought you were going to help. The way everyone avoids us or clams up when we're around, it's sure Daddy was *through* here at least. Why else should they be so secretive? Maybe they just don't want to get involved, but we've *got* to know. Don't you see?"

"I do." Hansl may have been the older of the two, but he was barely tall enough to look Mab in the eye. "I must tell you this: it is forbidden altogether that I speak with you. I disobey, but you will not tell Mama, please? Mama fears too much the evil that comes of stirring up the ghosts. There are old tales . . . it is said that the more you speak of them, the more of them there are."

Mab stared her amazement. "Do you believe all that stuff?"

Hansl raised his thin shoulders. "I do not know what to believe. Only that the ghosts do come in the deeps of winter. It is three winters now that Mama has seen one. When the moon is dark, always. She knows when they are stirring. By the headaches, you see. They are very fierce at such times."

A pleasurable shiver ran up Mab's spine. If there weren't Daddy to worry about, she would right then and there have sought out a quiet corner and pencil and paper and begun to spin the opening chapter of a horrid supernatural thriller. *They Walk in the Dark of the Moon.* No . . . *The Walkers in the Dark of the Moon?* That wasn't quite right either. She would have to remember to put it down in her notebook and work it out later. Now, pressing her nose against a pane of the door of the *Konditorei*, she waved violently, attracting the notice of a good half of the patrons before Perry, seated at the far table, caught sight of her grimaces and gulped down the last of his chocolate.

"Who was that you were sitting with?" asked Mab, as soon as the door closed behind her brother. "It looked like the friendly buzzard man. That Doctor-what's-his-name."

"Doktor Pfnür?" Hansl was impressed. "You have met Herr Doktor Pfnür? He is a very important man. Did he truly speak with you? He is director of the *Hochgebirgsschule*, the mountaineering school at the head of the valley. It is all that we have in Riesenmoos but the farming, now the tourists do not come."

Perry pushed Mab ahead of him, hurrying her down the path. "He just up and sat down by me. I guess he saw me holding my jaw—this stupid toothache—anyway, he asked me what the matter was, so I told him the filling's been throbbing like crazy off and on since yesterday. That's all. He's a nice enough old guy. Friendly. He wondered if the tooth needed refilling, because his dentist down in Pfarr-Werfen uses some new acrylic stuff that looks like tooth and doesn't show. But the ache was gone again and I told him, 'No, thanks.' Boy, you don't catch me going to the dentist twice in one month."

"M-maybe it's just this c-cold, and the filling's a kind of c-conductor," said Mab, her own teeth chattering.

Hansl, following behind, said nothing, but his brows drew together in a frown.

Hansl's friend Gabriel, a cheerful, blond young man in his mid-twenties, was delighted to enroll Mab and Perry in the intermediate ski class. "One day, two days only, what matter? Ach, you will *be* the intermediate class: the first class I have since coming to this job. When I have failed the advanced examination at the *Hochgebirgsschule*, I did not wish to leave Riesenmoos, and so here I am, doing nothing."

When Hansl had excused himself and hurried back to school, Gabriel Lanz put Mab and Perry through their paces on the nursery slope: snowplowing, stops, side-slipping, and (rather shaky) Christiana turns. Three winters' holidays at Big Bear and then Snow Valley and Aspen, had taught the children enough to keep them more or less vertical. Perry, despite his protests at anything resembling strenuous physical effort, had a natural talent: a "k-nack," as Gabriel pronounced it. Mab was absolutely fearless, but inclined to do things the hard way.

"Keep your bottom in to the hill as you turn," Gabriel yelled. "Edge your skis!"

From the nursery slope, Gabriel took the children out of the village to the Vogelerfeld, a slightly steeper hill-field with a tow-rope and longer runs. He kept up a steady stream of talk as they went, and only when the children were once again fastening on their skis, did they realize that they had not managed to get in a single question. They had learned next to nothing about the village, and very little about Mr. Lanz except that he had been in Riesenmoos since October and had spent a term at the Hochgebirgs-schule Pfnür learning elementary climbing techniques. They, on the other hand, had an uneasy suspicion that they had been very gently, amiably, and thoroughly pumped. If Gabriel knew anything about the "accident" up on the Tennen-gebirge, he must certainly have guessed the Birds' reason for being in the Eiswinkel, and also their lack of success in drawing information from the locals. He also knew now that Dr. Bird was a seismologist and Dr. Bachner a geologist; that Molly Bird, though she might not look it, was a very stubborn woman; and that Oriole was inclined to be bad-tempered at the breakfast table.

As Gabriel started the motor in the shed at the bottom of the drag lift, Mab thought she saw a furtive glance flicker toward Perry. "Sometimes," Gabriel said, straightening, "I think everyone here but young Hansl has forgot how to say more than '*Grüss Gott*' or '*Auf Wiedersehen.*' These Riesenmoosers are not friendly. Even my German grows rusty from the silence. It is a pleasure that you are come even for a few days. Perhaps I may teach your mother and sister too, *ja?* It is good for me to practice my English. I have a friend who works in summer on the Hollandisch packet boats that cross the English Channel, and he says that for me to obtain such a job good English will be of much help." The sharp look flickered again. "Two weeks past were two American gentlemen here, but they would speak only German with me, and they did not require skiing lessons."

Mab was a little puzzled, remembering that Hansl had mentioned Gabriel's spending a year in England. Doing what? And his English was pretty good—quite good enough for a summer job—except when he began talking about speaking English. Then his accent seemed to grow heavier and his speech more awkwardly deliberate. Or was it "deliberately awkward"? Suddenly, realizing *what* he had said, she forgot her suspicions in a rush of excitement. "Perry!" she squeaked.

"What's the matter with *you?*" Perry began. And then the words registered. "Americans? Two?"

Gabriel was singularly unhelpful. No, the gentlemen had

been too bundled up against the snow for him to describe them. One was tall, yes. But he had seen them only once. Yes, they could have been staying in a *pension,* but perhaps they had come and gone in a hired car. Nothing was sure.

"But it is sure that you will come tomorrow, is it not? For now we practice stemming a little here on the Vogelerfeld. Tomorrow, if you wish, we may go from the top of the field up and across through the forest to the end of the valley and around." He waved his arm to indicate the fields and wooded slopes below the lumpy line of limestone peaks that rimmed the Eiswinkel. "It is a good ski-touring. You must bring a lunch. Perhaps your mother and sister will enjoy also to come, as it is not to be lessons?"

"Why are you so interested in meeting Mama?" Mab asked abruptly, skewering Gabriel with a suspicious look. Molly Bird knew something about her husband's reasons for coming to Riesenmoos—something she had kept to herself. That could be what this young man was angling for. Mab hoped not. She had decided that she liked Gabriel Lanz just as speedily as she had decided that Byron Fleischacker was a clutz. Nice, but a clutz.

"Er—well, I am not. I mean, it is not exactly that I do not wish to meet your mother." Gabriel's eyes were a startling blue when they twinkled. He pulled off his stocking cap and ran a hand through his crisp blond curls. "I must confess it is your sister I would wish to meet. I have seen her in the middle of this morning taking coffee and a pastry in the Konditorei. She is very beautiful. If she does not belong to the mournful young man with the spectacles, you can persuade her perhaps to come tomorrow?"

"Maybe." Perry stumped off toward the drag lift, his expression clearly indicating that Gabriel had just come

44

down a good five or six notches in his estimation. Mab, however, by the time she had slithered to the top of the drag lift and come to rest in a snow bank, had already composed an affecting scene in which the Disguised Nobleman (G. Lanz) revealed his identity to the International Beauty (O. Bird) who had, in the guise of an humble tourist, nursed his broken body back to health after a Dreadful Accident in the wilds of somewhere-or-other. The exact nature of the dreadful accident had, however, to wait for pencil and paper and a private moment, since owing to the unexpected steepness of the Vogelerfeld, all of Mab's concentration was required to avoid a Dreadful Accident of her own.

The stemming went well. Gabriel admitted that Mab was perhaps a touch better on right-handed turns than left-handed ones; but he was very pleased with Perry. "Ach, if I could have you even for two weeks you would return to America ready for junior competition. But, as you do not know how long you stay . . . At least we will have tomorrow, yes?"

"Yes, please," said Mab. "And I'll see if Oriole will come." Having worked her romance-plot out a little further while watching Perry's last, swooping flight down the hill, Mab widened her eyes and smiled, all sweet innocence. "Actually, we're supposed to meet her at four at the Hotel Post. Would you like to come? We'll buy you a piece of cake."

Perry glowered. Mabbit was incurable. Here Gabriel had given them the first clue that might connect their father and Professor Bachner with Riesenmoos, and instead of concentrating on how valuable a Bird family outing with Gabriel as guide might be, she was weaving silly plots again. Like a fairy godmother in one of her kooky fairy tales.

45

"Yeah, we'll buy you a piece of cake," he said, as his hand went to his jaw. That was all he needed: the blankety-blank toothache was on again.

In the *Kaffeestube* of the Hotel Post, Oriole toyed with her rich chocolate Sachertorte, cutting it into tiny bites with her fork. Now and then she took a sip of coffee as she listened to the young man opposite with what she hoped was flattering attention. Herr Friml was a student at the Hochgebirgsschule Pfnür, a candidate for the First Certificate, which would qualify him for the much-coveted second year of study. "Last term," he explained earnestly, "two only from fifteen have survived the examination with a satisfactory score. The year before, only one. I do not complain about the so rigorous standards, you understand. I have no worry about the rope work and am quite good at the rappelling, but there are two—how do you say?—two 'vertical chimneys' on the test climb. Very difficult. So I must keep fit and make much exercise for the thighs and arms. Most of the trainees, you see, are older and larger than I. That is why I have ordered the *gulyas* soup instead of the cake. More nourishing. But you, Fräulein—will you have more coffee?"

Herr Friml was very blond, scrubbed, and pink-cheeked; and if his conversation was overly concerned with Herr Friml, at least he was more interesting than Herr Lederer, the woodcutter, or Herr Thurner, the baker. Old Herr Glöckner, the church sexton, with whom she and Byron and Byron's tape recorder had spent the early afternoon, had added only a little ghostly lore to a growing collection of ancient gossip. But half an hour ago the disheartened Byron had been introduced to Father Sepp, the parish priest, who, as it turned out, had a handwritten copy of the old Carnival play. So far as Oriole knew, Byron was still tucked away in the church's tiny muniments room, deaf to the world, poring over moldy books and documents and muttering, as he had to her, "If only I can find the *old* play itself!" Father Sepp's copy clearly had been transcribed from a very old source, but it was incomplete, Byron insisted.

Still, Oriole's day need not be a total loss. She leaned her chin on her hands and, taking a deep breath, turned on a melting smile. "No more coffee, thank you. But I could listen for *hours*. I think mountain-climbing must be terribly exciting. Do you have much time for exploring on your own? I was wondering if there were still more peaks beyond the ridge on this side of the valley."

Young Herr Friml smiled tolerantly at her ignorance. "*Ach*, no, Fräulein. It is a great plateau and very wild. Some of the staff and third-year men know it well, I think, but it is off-bounds to us first-year men." Abruptly, his voice wavered. "Actually," he said, swallowing nervously, "at this hour the Hotel Post also is off limits, as I have this moment remembered. You will please to excuse me? You are most kind. *Auf Wiedersehen, gnadige Fräulein.*"

In a flash he was gone. Oriole, thwarted in what could have been a promising line of investigation, looked around in bewilderment. The timid Herr Friml had bounded away like a rabbit who has suddenly caught a whiff of weasel, but no one in the almost empty coffee-room had an even faintly weaselish air. Two school-teacherly ladies were unwinding over *Kugelhupf* and coffee; a tidy gentleman, who might have been either a post-office clerk or a teller in the tiny village bank (or both, as they occupied the same office), sipped at a glass of red wine; and a thickset, pudding-faced woman with a mannish haircut and a fuzzy green tweed suit had just paid her bill and was drawing on her gloves.

"You looking for us, Orry? Here we are." Mab appeared at her sister's elbow, red-nosed and cherry-cheeked, with an amused Gabriel in tow. Plumping down on the red leather seat, she slid into the far end of the booth. "Oriole Bird meet Gabriel Lanz," she announced. "Gabriel Lanz, Oriole Bird."

"*Oriole* Bird?" Gabriel looked from Mab to Oriole. "You are pulling my leg, yes?"

"Unfortunately, no," Oriole answered. But her weighed-down-by-the-weight-of-it-all look did not last long in the face of Gabriel's admiring stare. "Um, ah—Mab? Where is Perry?" she asked, flustered.

"Off buying some aspirin. He'll be here in a minute. Guess what? We had a ski lesson, and Gabriel says we can go off cross-country tomorrow. How would you . . ."

The fuzzy green tweed woman passed their booth, nodding pleasantly to Gabriel as she went by. As soon as the doors into the lobby had stopped swinging, Oriole leaned across the table. "Who was that?" she whispered to Gabriel. "A minute ago I was talking to one of the mountain-climbers, and something made him take off like a shot. Someone he saw, I think. It couldn't have been those two little old spinsters in the corner . . ."

". . . or the old-maidish gentleman with the mustache." Gabriel finished for her. "You are right. The green lady is our esteemed Doktor Klara Nussdorf—Frau Pfnür. Herr Doktor Pfnür is the director of the climbing school, but it is his good lady who oversees the students' diet and discipline. She is—" He paused as if reaching for the right word, but it occurred to both girls that he had changed his mind about what he had been going to say. "She is a dragon about the taking of vitamins and keeping to schedules. Perhaps at this hour the students are to be in their quarters studying the Theory of Climbing. It would be no wonder that your friend fled."

"Oh, he's not a friend," Oriole said hastily. Recovering her composure, she said primly, "How interesting about Mrs. Pfnür. You said 'Doktor.' Is she a medical doctor?"

The laugh-crinkles around Gabriel's eyes deepened and then disappeared as he answered solemnly. "I think not. At least, she does not practice medicine here. Perhaps she is, like her husband, a Doctor of Philosophy. But Riesenmoos does not care about such things. It is enough that the Pfnürs provide summer jobs for many woodcutters and that their students bring a little extra money into the village in these hard times."

"Where's Byron, Orry?" asked Mab, changing the subject artfully. The Pfnürs were not half so interesting as her own plot, which, though off to a promising start, was in need of a slight nudge. "What did you two do all day?"

Gabriel's ears pricked up noticeably, but Oriole was saved—temporarily—from her small sister's machinations by a sudden hubbub in the lobby, in the midst of which a breathless Byron came bursting through the swinging doors into the *Kaffeestube*.

"I say!" he panted. "Maybe you'd better come out here, Oriole. There's somebody trying to kidnap young Peregrine!"

49

five

"I HAVE NEVER BEEN SO EMBARRASSED IN MY ENTIRE *life*," declaimed Oriole for the twentieth time—the third since sitting down to breakfast in the cozy dining alcove of the Strumpf parlor. She affected great interest in the colorful rooster pattern of the window curtains and pointedly avoided looking at Perry. "Absolutely *never*."

"Oh, dry up," grumbled Perry. "You'd think it was an international incident, the way you come on."

Kani Strumpf finished his bowl-sized cup of *Kapuziner* coffee and carefully wiped his mustache with a red-and-white checkered napkin. "*Ach*, it was a small misunderstanding. By this morning the good Doktor Pfnür and his Frau will have forgot. You must also." Rising, he excused himself hurriedly, as if the strain of stringing so many foreign words together in one speech had proved too much for him. A moment later, he could be heard in the hallway, stoking up the shiny brown-tile parlor stove through the "cupboard door" that neatly concealed the stoke-hole.

"The whole thing was as much your Byron's fault as Perry's," defended Mab stoutly. "If Perry says it was an accident Dr. Pfnür got kicked in the shin, then it was. I'll bet you'd kick too if perfect strangers tried to cart you off to the dentist willy-nilly. Well, she *would*, Mama. Anyhow, it was Byron who made the big scene, thinking old Piggy was *having* to struggle to get out of the car."

Mrs. Bird buttered another *croissant*. "What I still fail to understand is what you were doing in the Pfnürs' car in the first place, Perry. If you had no intention of accepting a ride to the dentist, why get in at all?"

Perry's brow creased. He shrugged. "I dunno. It just sort of seemed the thing to do at the time. I don't remember why. I remember Mrs. Pfnür saying she was taking him— Dr. P.—down to catch the train for Salzburg and could drop me by the dentist's and pick me up later. I guess she was kind of convincing. Or else the toothache sort of numbed me in the head."

"I don't like the sound of that tooth at all," said Mrs. Bird. "I really ought to take you into Salzburg and have it seen to."

"No, no. It's all gone now," Perry hastened to protest. "Anyhow, it hardly ever lasts more than half an hour, off and on. Yesterday when the toothache stopped, I guess I sort of felt all closed in in that little car. I had to get out quick."

"You didn't have to yell 'Help!'" Oriole was still in the sullens. "It wasn't Byron's fault. What was he supposed to think? Honestly, Mama, half the village came running. They all looked at us as if they positively hated us, and heaven knows they weren't exactly falling all over themselves to welcome us before. The Pfnürs are *terribly* important here."

Mrs. Bird sighed. "I know. Frau Strumpf wouldn't even say '*Guten Morgen*' when I came down just now. I'm beginning to wonder if we did the right thing in coming here. Yesterday I found out exactly nothing from the women I spoke to in the village. I simply *hate* being buffaloed like this. I hate feeling helpless. But we can't give it up. I *won't* give up, not after your friend Gabriel's 'two Americans,' but if we don't find some trace of your father soon, I won't know what to *do*. You must keep your eyes open on this outing of yours this morning. I'll explore the valley and hope for an inspiration. There are several outlying farms I haven't pestered with my questions yet." In a thoughtful, but utterly matter-of-fact tone, she added, alarmingly, "I'm *sure* Jeffrey isn't far from here. Last night I dreamed that he was close by and in danger. It was very dark, so I couldn't see . . ."

She trailed off into her own thoughts, and the table lapsed into an unhappy silence broken only by the sounds of eating, of china and cutlery. Mab took up the bread knife to trim an article out of the latest *Herald-Tribune:* an article headlining a brief but sharp tremor centered twelve miles from Ravenna, in Italy. The disturbance had been predicted, it said,

". . . with an error of only ten miles, and within one degree of its reading of 4 on the Richter scale of 10: a nearly pinpoint accuracy which only last year, at the time of the San Fernando earthquake near Los Angeles, Caltech seismologists were saying would not be attainable for some years. Italian officials have expressed deep gratitude for the warning provided by Seismological Forecasting. They were given sufficient warning to take steps protecting the city's treasures, most particularly the priceless tile mosaics on the walls of the ancient Byzantine church of San Vitale: mosaics which otherwise would have been seriously endangered. Seismological Forecasting is a division of the Earthquake Control and Modification Research Center of Antelope Valley, California . . ."

Into the breakfast-table silence strode big, sad-faced Kani Strumpf. He came in from the hallway with a thick, cream-colored envelope, addressed in a scrawl of brown ink, held gingerly between his thumb and forefinger, and gave a small, courtly bow as he handed this missive to Mrs. Bird. Usually expressionless, he managed to look almost friendly.

"For you, Frau Bird. From Frau Doktor Pfnür. It was brought by one of the young men from the Hochgebirgs-schule, who waits now in the hall for a reply."

The children crowded close as their mother slit the en-velope with her buttery knife and pulled out a folded sheet of expensive notepaper. On it, Frau Pfnür offered a gracious apology for the previous afternoon's misunderstanding, and an invitation to tea for the Bird children. There would be a personally conducted tour of the training school, followed by refreshments. "If this prospect pleases the little ones, the autobus of the Hochgebirgsschule will collect them at three of the clock p.m." It was signed *Klara Nussdorf Pfnür*, *Doctor of Philosophy* (*Göttingen*).

"Very impressive." Mrs. Bird's eyebrows quirked up into her Crafty Gypsy look. "You and I must not rate, Oriole. Still, it *is* thoughtful of Frau Pfnür, and it may be our only chance to learn something about these mountains and the plateau beyond. The staff and students would know if there have been avalanches up there. They might even have seen some sign of Jeffrey and Gus's explorations."

"Do we *have* to go? I'll feel pretty silly going over there after all that gefuffle yesterday," Perry objected. "Besides, we're going ski-touring with Gabriel Lanz. Mab's already got Hansl to ask his mother to make us sandwiches for lunch."

Oriole gave a little "Hmph!" of disapproval. "You can certainly be back in time to change before three o'clock. After all, you're the one who should be apologizing, not Frau Pfnür." Her frown vanished suddenly. "Perhaps I ought to go with you to make sure you don't go putting your foot in it again. After all, I am one of the 'Bird children' even if I'm not a child. That is, if you don't think it will be an imposition, Mama," she added earnestly, ignoring Mab's cross-eyed smirk.

"Besides, there will be all those muscle-men doing exercises and Starved for the Sight of a Female," Mab put in nastily. Gabriel's chances were dwindling rapidly. After all, he had flunked out of the climbing school.

"No, no." Mrs. Bird answered Oriole's question vaguely as she scribbled a note of acceptance on a post card carried off from the Österreichischer Hof Hotel in Salzburg. "There." She handed the card to Herr Strumpf, and he carried it into the hall. "Now." She folded her napkin. "I must ask Frau Strumpf if she will make up a lunch for me as well. I don't suppose the last of the farmers' wives will tell me any more than the first, but just the same, I'll finish making my rounds."

"Mama?" Oriole spoke with an elaborately casual air

that made Mab look up from the *Trib*'s description of the disastrous floods in Monza and Padua in northern Italy. "Mama," Oriole said, "don't you think I should go along with Mab and Perry on this outing with their ski instructor, too? I mean, we don't really know anything about the young man, this Gerald What's-his-name, do we?"

"Gabriel. Gabriel Lanz," Mab said dryly. Oriole knew his name perfectly well, but it might be more politic not to say so. And having it Oriole's own idea was better than asking her to come along. She folded the newspaper and scraped her chair back. "I'll tell Hansl's mother two more lots of sandwiches."

Mrs. Bird, raising an eyebrow at Mab's satisfied tone, gave Oriole a speculative look, which Oriole was fortunately too preoccupied to notice.

"Cross-country?" Byron shaded his eyes from the sun's glare with a gloved hand and peered at Oriole. "With him? —I mean, them?" He gestured toward Gabriel and the children, busy fastening their ski bindings, and said plaintively, "I thought you were going to spend the day with me. I have to get Herr Glöckner to tell his 'Ice Brides' stories over again. That tape is full of skips and blank spots somehow. Then . . ." He hesitated. "After that I rather hoped you might help me look through the old parish records for references to the old *Eisschemenlaufen*. It's tremendously exciting, this historical detection. 'An history mystery,' you might say." His eyes gleamed. "Father Sepp's 'original' copy of the playlet has to have been copied about two hundred years ago from an even older one. You can tell from the handwriting. But I suppose that sounds dull to you," he said suddenly. He glowered at Gabriel Lanz, who only stamped his skis experimentally, shrugged a compact knapsack over his shoulders, buckling its third strap across his broad chest, and politely pretended not to have heard.

Perry, turning his back on such adult nonsense, went clumping up the road toward the Vogelerfeld lift. Mab, enjoying Oriole's discomfiture, hung back. Sooner or later Oriole had to catch on that a good half of Byron's melting look of devotion was near-sightedness. If she weren't so contrary she would see that though Byron might be tall, dark, and even handsome (with his glasses off), beside Gabriel's solidity and amused reserve he seemed very young for the advanced age of twenty-two.

"Now you *know* it doesn't sound dull to me, Byron. I would adore to help you make your . . . your Major Discovery, but—" Oriole's voice dropped to a confiding whisper. "We think Mr. Lanz actually saw Daddy some time before the accident. It's best not to mention it to anyone because Daddy was on a . . . a sort of confidential mission. You won't say anything, will you? You see, there are a lot of questions I must ask Mr. Lanz." She wrinkled her nose as if it were a bothersome chore.

Mab's hopes for a scene were disappointed. She began, in fact, to be a little uneasy. Oriole, for all her preachment about utter frankness, had a disconcertingly deft hand with the soft soap. When Byron admitted reluctantly that perhaps it was for the best because, "It's queer, but these people do seem to open up to me more when I'm on my own than when you're with me," his frown had all but disappeared. A dazzling smile, a promise of dinner and a sleigh ride after, and a reassured Byron was off to his researches with a bounce to his step.

Mab, hurrying after Perry and Gabriel, wondered if

56

Oriole's avowed intentions of keeping them out of mischief, and of coming along to check out Gabriel's qualifications and general trustworthiness concealed her own little plot? To change Gabriel's amused appreciation to something more like Byron's uncritical devotion? Oriole was used to being taken seriously.

No matter. Whatever Oriole's intentions, they were forgotten between the bottom and the top of the Vogelerfeld lift. The morning was bright, the air clear, and the deep little valley of the Eiswinkel, open as it was to the south, sparkled like a cupful of sunshine. Below and to the right, Riesenmoos itself was a fairy-tale village, a little knot of crooked streets tied around the mustard-colored church with its needle-pointed spire. Outlying farmhouses, dots on the shining white fields, sent up thin tendrils of smoke from busy kitchens. Even questions about the strangers Gabriel claimed to have seen were forgotten in the exhilaration of the view and of breathing out great clouds of frosty air.

Gabriel had brought skins for everyone's skis—strips of hide to be worn on the underside of the ski, the fur side next to the snow. "You have not used skins before? I show you now, then." Unfastening his skis, Gabriel stood them upright in the snow. "It slips on, so; and fastens, so. The— how do you call it?—the 'grain'? No, the 'nap.' The nap of the hairs must lie smooth from front to back to give the traction. The hairs, you see, are ruffled up when your weight pushes a little backwards, and they make the walking up the slope more easy, so. Going downhill, when the weight is forward, they slick back and do not slow you more than a little. I prefer them to bothering with special waxes."

Snapping shut the second cable fastener and buckling the loose safety strap that fastens ski to boot, he took several

57

quick strides uphill to the nearest trees. "You see?" he called. "With the skins you do not slip back at every step —unless it is very steep, of course. Come, try them. Yes, Perry, good. Very good. No, no, little Mab. Remember that your poles are of no help if you thrust them ahead so. *Ja*, better. *Ach*, Miss Bird—Oriole—you have forgot your safety strap, the left one. But you move very good. Yes, indeed, very good." He cleared his throat. "Now: we will go upward through the forest from here half a mile by the track the woodcutters use. It is an easy climb."

It was not a difficult climb, and in the deep-shadowed forest not such warm work as it would have been in the sunshine; but Mab, being much the smallest, had a hard pull of it. The ancient wagon track angled gradually but steadily up the slope, a dim white road through the black pines.

After the first few hundred yards, Mab had to stop and bend over to catch her breath. As the others moved on, she looked around, shivering in the chill air that had seemed warm enough so long as she was moving, but now felt like needles of ice in her lungs. The stillness was so deep that it seemed to Mab the only sound in the wild wood was her own breathing. The sun that shone so brightly out in the wide world found not even a chink to shine through here, and the light under the great shaggy trees was like the gray-green gloom of late afternoon.

It was eerie, Mirkwoody. "I sure wouldn't want to be in here after dark," she thought, adding aloud, "but I don't believe in your old ice-giant-ghosts!" Nonetheless, in the chill gloom she looked uneasily over her shoulder. Her teeth chattered; and with a sudden spurt of energy she swung after the others, who had disappeared through the trees.

Before long the climbing black pines thinned. Perry, Oriole, and Gabriel could be seen higher and far ahead, near a ragged outcropping of rock. They leaned on their ski poles, waiting patiently. At least, Perry and Gabriel waited patiently. Oriole, predictably, was wringing her hands. Mab, as soon as she was in earshot, wheezed out, "Man, I thought that last goblin had me for sure!"

"Goblin?" Oriole fixed her with a doubtful and then a horrified stare. "Someone was following you? Oh, Mabbit, who was it? Did you see? I should never have let you out of my sight. What if something perfectly awful had happened?"

Gabriel smothered an impolite grin, but Perry was less tactful. "Don't be such a dreary old doom-seer, Orry. She's only pulling your leg. You ought to know she hardly ever *isn't.*"

"It is not difficult from here on, little Mab," Gabriel reassured her. "Catch your breath, take off your skins, and from here we go soaring." From his knapsack he drew a heavy pair of field glasses and set to scanning the valley. Below, the forest dropped steeply away. The village had fallen far below and behind. Only Haus Strumpf, higher than the others, was not completely hidden by trees. They had come about halfway along the valley and could see that its upper end was deeply wooded at the lower levels, but then climbed steeply and barely up and away toward the looming peaks. It was those slopes that Gabriel, after a perfunctory sweep of the valley, scanned most carefully.

Perry was curious. "Why the glasses? What are you looking for?"

"Birds," said the young man obscurely. After a while he

murmured, "I thought I saw a hawk. I must have been mistaken. Most intelligent birds are wintering on the Mediterranean."

Oriole and Mab looked at each other. Birds or *Birds?*

Perry didn't notice anything. "Can I have a look?" Accepting the glasses, he focused on a tiny dot moving along the faraway ribbon of road below. "Man, these are powerful! There: it *is* Mom. She's going the same direction we are." He passed the glasses to Oriole. "Down along the stream. She's above the last farm, just past where the road goes over the bridge."

Mab took the glasses after Oriole's brief look. She located the tiny, great-coated, fur-hatted figure and then followed the wriggle of the road and stream on up the valley. "She won't get much further. There's a gate up there where the woods start."

"*Ja*. It is the approach to the Hochgebirgsschule—the Pfnürschule, the trainees call it. You cannot see the school itself from here, but we go to the other side of the valley, from where you will see. Have you caught your breath, little one? From here it is a nice, long run. Ups and downs, yes, but most are coasting-ups, not climbing ones." He stowed the binoculars in his knapsack, slipped it on again, and with the warning, "Follow closely," pushed off.

"Whoo-ee!" Perry grinned shakily. "That last little old bit was kind of hairy, wasn't it?" Oriole, trying to be nonchalant, hid her trembling knees by reclining casually against a weathered fragment of criss-cross fence that had once been a rick for drying hay. Mab, once her skis were off and planted upright in the snow, flopped back full length and with a great sigh flapped her arms to make angel wings in the snow.

"Flying! That was like flying," she croaked. "My knees feel like Jello, and I won't ever be able to stand up again, but who cares!"

Gabriel regarded all three approvingly. "You have done well. But please, what is 'hairy'?"

"Risky. Scary-dangerous," Perry offered. "That stretch between the two climbing trails at the head of the valley—man, once over the edge, and that's a lo-o-ng step down."

"*Ja, vielleicht.* But it is so short a bit. And with a nice fat ledge a hundred yards wide, who needs to step over?"

"A nice fat sloping ledge," Oriole accused.

"It was lovely," Mab croaked. She sat up. "But maybe we *had* better go back another way."

Gabriel laughed. "*Ja.* We will make a long, easy run of it down this side of the valley and cross the Riesenbach at the bridge below the Mooserkreuz. But first we eat and enjoy. We must use up the four hours you are paying for, no?" He slipped his rucksack off and propped it upright in the snow. When he spoke again, it was with regret. "It will be too bad when you go. I think Herr Metzger must be firing me soon. When there are no skiers for the ski school, he does not have to pay me, but now I think Frau Metzger grows tired of feeding me.

Everyone set about unpacking lunches, opening Thermoses, and unwrapping sandwiches made with crusty rolls. Gabriel bit into a sausage roll and looked the three Birds over thoughtfully. Finally he seemed to come to a decision and, pointing back the way they had come, said, "From here you can see the Pfnürschule. There—it shelters against the cliff at the top of the valley."

"*That's* our 'nice fat ledge'? That bitty strip above the cliff?" Mab clapped a dramatic hand to her forehead and fell back onto the snow in a mock faint.

Gabriel smiled briefly. "The training students use the cliff for practice in rappelling—descending on a double rope—and the trails there which I pointed out to you climb over the saddle to the Luftkogel Pass. There is no climbing now, though. It is said to be a dangerous avalanche area and is closed until after the spring thaws."

"And you brought us across just there, below the saddle?" Oriole was incredulous. "Why, that ledge runs right across an avalanche funnel!"

Gabriel's smile was calm. His blue eyes held hers. "It is a curious thing. Beyond the saddle is said to be very dangerous, with many small slides on the high couloirs every day that the sun shines; but never down on this side. So much snow hangs above the Pfnürschule, but never has there been even the smallest snowslide until after the spring thaws are well under way. Doesn't that seem curious to you?"

"But—"

"Riesenmoosers say that the giants prowl up there, fighting great snow battles among themselves. Avalanches and ice giants. Two good stories to keep men off the mountains of the Eiswinkel, no? There are other curiosities too." From his rucksack Gabriel brought out another sausage roll, and the heavy field glasses, which he handed to Oriole. He pointed across the valley. "Follow north along the *Schneide*—the crest—from the Königskogel. Do you see the sharper peak, perhaps two-thirds of the way along? Past the little *col*. Yes, now straight down. No, up a little again. There is a steep-sided gully."

"Yes, I see. Why . . ." Oriole touched the focus wheel. "Back in there—Is that a cave?" Her nose wrinkled as she squinted. "It's the Eisschemenhöhle, isn't it?"

Gabriel didn't flicker an eyelash, but it was a moment before he said, "Yes. How do you know that? It isn't in any guide book."

"Herr Glöckner, the little man who takes care of the church, told me. Byron and me, that is." Oriole lowered the glasses, passing them to Mab. "The Ice Brides. That was it. The Eisschemenhöhle is where they all disappeared. Herr Glöckner remembers his great-grandmother telling stories about them she heard as a girl."

"Tell us," said Gabriel. For the first time he looked at her with something more than amused appreciation.

"There were a number of different stories," Oriole explained. "But in all of them a village maiden falls in love with a handsome stranger who lures her up to the cave. It's always a deep, harsh winter, and always on a moonlit night. When she doesn't come back, the villagers are afraid to go up to look before the winter's over. It's the same in every story. Come spring, the villagers would go into the cave as far as the first chamber, and there would be a new ice column that hadn't been there before. They thought it was the girl, you see. Herr Glöckner says that the last time it's supposed to have happened was sometime in the eighteenth century. That was when people began taking offerings up to the cave at Carnival time—meat and bread and salt, things like that—and the food seemed to pacify the giants as well as the maidens had."

"Not very intelligent of them," murmured Gabriel under his breath.

"But how cool!" was Mab's comment as she handed the glasses on to an impatient Perry. Seeing his pained look, she grinned. "I meant the story, idiot, not the icy maidens." To Oriole, she observed with a wicked air of innocence, "Orry, do you suppose Herr Glöckner might have been trying to scare you off a little bit?"

"Scare me off? Off what?" Oriole was unsuspecting. The answer—"handsome strangers"—dawned on her as Perry whooped and Gabriel struggled against a smile.

"I think that your little sister asks for a snow bath," Gabriel said mildly. "But that will wait. I am most interested to hear of these 'Ice Brides.' Such stories help to explain how sensible folk can believe in nonsensical demons. If you hear such tales from the time you are small . . ." He frowned. "About the cave itself—legend says that all of the caverns in these mountains are connected like a great honeycomb of chambers: the Eisriesenwelt, the Eiskogelhöhle, the Eisschemenhöhle, and the smaller ones. It is not known whether this is true, for much is still unexplored. The Eisschemenhöhle itself has been closed for two hundred years. Your tale of the brides perhaps explains why the cave has been shut up and fallen almost out of memory, but I have it in my head that you may have the answer, too, to the riddle of the trail that climbs up beyond it and over the ridge."

"Me? Us?" Oriole stared.

"Ja. The trail is on no map, the Pfnürschule never uses it, and there has been not a footprint on it all the year until a fortnight ago, though it is so old and deeply worn that its mark is clear among the trees and even up into the rocks. For these reasons, I was mystified two weeks ago to be sitting here and see two men go up it, over the top, and come down again only an hour later. One wore a white anorak—a 'windbreaker,' you call it?—and a red knitted cap, as did one of the strangers I have seen in the village at that time. That startles you? Perhaps, then, you might guess what purpose these men could have in crossing the ridge?"

"Daddy!" Mab's whisper rose to a shriek. "It was our daddy!"

"So I have been thinking. What I should like to know is the why of it. It is a mystery, no? Something he thought to discover there, *ja?*"

"How should we know?" Perry was suddenly cautious. "And why didn't you tell us all this before?"

Gabriel shrugged. He avoided Oriole's look of bewilderment and accusation. "It was necessary not to be overheard. Riesenmoos is a strange place. It seems to have agreed that your papa and his friend did not exist, and since I stay on sufferance only, I pretend to this agreement despite my curiosity. And now it would seem that you know no more than I, *hein?* I have wished today to persuade you, please, to remove your mother and yourselves to Salzburg or, better still, to America. And now I must think it even more necessary that you leave. It is no wisdom to blunder into a mystery for which you have no key." He smiled faintly. "Your mother is a very determined lady, I think. It is to be seen in the way she puts her feet down as she walks. But she must be made to understand that it is impossible that anyone should survive even twenty-four hours up on the plateau in such bad weather as we had two weeks ago. It is very easy up there in snow or mist to lose your way. It was not known here in Riesenmoos that the two gentlemen were missing, I am sure, or the

Alpine Rescue Service would have been called in the search. I cannot believe that . . ."

"How could it *not* be known? Why weren't they reported missing?" Oriole cried. "What's the *matter* with this place? We can't even find out where they were staying."

"What is the matter with Riesenmoos? It is a good question," said the young man grimly. "I have no answer. Something in the air, perhaps. And Riesenmoos is more of a puzzle than you may know. Have you noticed how the younger children are small and spindly? This is so only here in the Eiswinkel, and among the adults the valley has the highest rate of nervous collapse in the whole of Austria. I—well, I have been curious, and have looked up statistics in these matters. It was not always so. These past few years much has changed. The people do not sing now, though once they were famous for their choirs. The cows no longer give milk in the winter, and the goats will not suckle their kids. The post-bus must bring milk and butter from Werfenweng each day in wintertime. All these troubles and more; and yet no one leaves." He shrugged. "I have puzzled over these things as you have puzzled over your papa's coming here, but it is fruitless. If there are answers, they are well and truly hidden."

"Anything that's hidden can be found." Mab was defiant. "We aren't going to give up just on your say-so."

Gabriel handed Oriole a handkerchief for the sniffles she could not stop. "I wish you would," he said gravely. "I like you all very much."

"Oh? You certainly seem intent on getting rid of us," Oriole said with a bitter glance and a final sniffle. "But you might as well save your breath. We aren't leaving. The

66

children may be too inexperienced, but Mama and I have done enough climbing in the Sierras to be able to go up that trail and see whatever it was Daddy went to see. We'll *have* to."

Gabriel objected with unexpected violence. "Impossible! The trail is unbroken since last week's blizzard. The snow is too deep and the going too heavy for a woman. Even with a guide, the plateau is a dangerous wilderness. You cannot—"

Perry had been unusually silent, scarcely listening as he stared out across the valley with the field glasses. Now he broke in suddenly. "Gabriel? You said nobody ever goes up to the cave, but somebody sure as heck is now. And if it's who I think it is, the track has to be pretty clear. At least the lower part . . . *Hey!*"

Gabriel snatched the binoculars so abruptly that Perry teetered over on his side in the snow. Focusing quickly, the young man located the climbers Perry had spotted. Then, frowning thoughtfully, he passed the glasses automatically to Oriole. She in turn peered briefly through them and turned them over to Mab.

"Children. Those are children," Oriole puzzled. "Unless they're dwarfs. *Nothing* would be surprising in this idiotic place."

"They are children, all right." Gabriel shook his head. "Hansl I know by the long orange scarf, and there are— eight others. It is knapsacks, I think, that give them the hunched-over look. But I do not understand. What can they be doing?"

Mab squinted. The tiny figures struggling upward from the forest were too far away for being sure, but it looked as if they also carried baskets or boxes, singly or between two smaller children. The nearer they drew to the cleft that led to the cave's entrance, the more strung-out the line grew. The tiny orange-scarfed figure in the lead deposited his burden in the snow and moved down to help the littlest and last. Mab touched the focus gear gingerly. The glasses were so heavy that she had a hard time holding them steady on the object Hansl had left beside the trail and was now retrieving. It looked like the same deep, round basket she had seen him packing while his mother made the ham and cheese sandwiches for the Birds' lunches.

Gabriel reached for the glasses to stow them away again. "Come. Put your skis on quickly. We are going down. I must find out what that rascal of a Hansl is up to."

"Halfway there," said Perry, struggling with his second ski.

"Don't fall all over yourself," said Mab. "If you just want to know what it is he's doing, he's taking a basketload of food up there. Bread and salt, canned peaches, brown eggs, even a tube of condensed milk. I saw him packing it all up after breakfast."

"*Food?*" Oriole's gloomy mood evaporated. "But that's incredible. They *can't* be making propitiatory offerings to ice demons in this day and age, can they? How absolutely medieval! Poor Byron will be beside himself. He's been hoping for a genuine 'superstitious survival,' and he's missed seeing it happen." She busied herself with her ski bindings. "Still, he can explain it all to us."

"That will be nice," Gabriel Lanz said drily.

six

"Just you wait, Hansl Strumpf." Mab was still thinking dark thoughts about Hansl's expedition, though why he should have told her about it, she could not have said. Neither he nor Mrs. Bird had returned to Haus Strumpf by the time the VW bus from the Pfnürschule arrived at three o'clock to pick up Oriole and the children. But Hansl had to come home sometime, and when he did . . .

For now, Mab sedately followed Oriole and young Herr Friml over the threshold of the Hochgebirgsschule Pfnür, and the high, beamed entrance hall of the mountain training school effectively put the mystery of the Eisschemenhöhle out of her mind. She had never seen such a room. Silk banners with the insignia of the Austrian provinces hung from black, carved beams, and dim paintings of determined-looking men and wild mountain scenery peered down from dark paneled walls. Rich Caucasian rugs warmed the flagstone floor, and a crackling fire in the huge fireplace made the great dim room seem cozy and welcoming.

Herr Doktor Pfnür himself greeted the visitors, unfolding his bony length from a comfortable overstuffed chair. Exuding warmth and welcome, he thanked the good luck and good weather that had allowed him to finish his business in Vienna and return by the early train. Frau Pfnür, regrettably, had several urgent business letters to write, but would join them later. The Doktor inquired after Perry's toothache, was glad to hear that it was no longer giving trouble, and professed himself delighted that Oriole had accompanied her young brother and sister. "These halls are too rarely graced by beautiful young ladies," said he as he kissed her hand.

Oriole was a little startled, but it was done so elegantly she decided she rather liked it, and in return managed a polite "How wonderful it is to find such an imposing building in the back-of-beyond. It's not the least bit like a school."

"That is because you come when many of my young men are away. We arrange our terms so that during our avalanche season we are not cooped up together in forced inactivity. But you may meet some of our staff. I myself am to give you the grand tour." He rubbed his hands together in benevolent enthusiasm. "We shall see everything, and Peregrine and Mavis must not feel shy about plying me with questions. Agreed? Excellent. If you will come this way?" Slipping a hand under Oriole's elbow, he guided the little group toward the old-fashioned elevator—rather like a fancy Victorian birdcage—at the far end of the hall.

Twenty or thirty doors later, they had still seen only a part of the school, which, as Doktor Pfnür explained, had been built as a hotel in 1890 by a wealthy brewer with a taste for romantic Gothic castles. Year after year the brewer had added here a turret, there a wing, and in the end the hotel had never opened, for the brewery's profits had been drained dry before the last of the roof was on. Despite the presence of his ghost, which was said to pace the halls, planning new splendors, the roofed portion had for a number of years housed a sanitarium for consumptives. Not long after World War II that venture also withered away, and the old building stood empty until the Pfnürs, on a walking tour, discovered it in 1966.

"Is it? Haunted, I mean." Mab peered curiously around the *Rittersaal*, the Knights' Hall, that served both as dining hall and the main lecture-room for the students. Thickets of antlers bristled high on the walls, and above the head table loomed *Die Bergkameraden*, a very large and very sentimental painting of two heroic young climbers saluting the Königskogel with their ice axes.

Like the recreation and dormitory rooms tucked along the crooked upstairs corridors and opening off steep circular staircases, the *Rittersaal* was furnished very plainly. Except for the cheerful front hall, the Pfnürschule watchword appeared to be Utility, not Comfort. The few trainees the children had seen were industriously greasing climbing boots, darning socks, or poring over maps and manuals. The one or two who looked to be older, the children took to be instructors. But there was no chance to talk with anyone as Mrs. Bird had suggested. Doktor Pfnür kept up a steady stream of explanation and anecdote.

"Haunted? Dear child, what an amusing notion! No, I fear that even if these halls had their midnight visitants, we are such practical and sadly unimaginative souls that they would not bother to appear to us. Once we had roofed and repaired the unfinished west wing, our first year here, we shut out the wind and with it all our ghostly sounds. But perhaps you have been listening to our innocent friends down in the village. To see ghosts one must believe that there are mysteries beyond our reach." He wagged a playful finger. "For us, it is not so. The motto of the Hochgebirgsschule Pfnür is *Immer ans Höchst erreichen:* 'To reach always for the highest.' We do not admit that anything lies beyond our reach." Despite the smile and the wagging finger, it sounded oddly ominous.

After the *Rittersaal* came the equipment room, where snowshoes, ski sticks, ice axes, and trim coils of rope hung in geometrical patterns on the walls, like weapons in a medieval armory. Skis stood in ranks in special racks. Perry was fascinated, but also a bit puzzled by the arrangement, which seemed more concerned with effect than efficiency. Numbered first-aid kits and cartons of sunburn cream in precise stacks filled one small cupboard, and in wooden trays on open shelves *karabiners*, plain pitons, *Knöchelschutzen* to protect the ankles, bootlaces, and packets of ski wax, and other small items were arranged with military neatness. They were all faintly dusty, but then it was the school's slack season.

Mab was more impressed by the huge kitchen where a great smoke-stained fireplace—complete with bake-oven, spits, and a cheerful fire—was flanked by a shiny three-oven stainless steel range, and the walls were hung with all sizes of gleaming copper pots and pans. She and Perry watched, mouths watering, as the cook slid from an oven two large trays of fresh-baked *Tascherln*—Viennese jam pockets—and the jelly doughnuts known as *Faschingskrapfen,* the traditional treat for the week before Lent. It was almost too much to bear.

"Hang in there, Old Pig," whispered Mab solemnly as Doktor Pfnür led Oriole toward yet another door. "Only fifty-five rooms to go."

Perry rolled his eyes and clutched his stomach. "I'll never make it. Not if he keeps on showing us every broom closet and linen cupboard."

"Every closet and cupboard" was an exaggeration, but considering the bare sameness of so many of the rooms, it did seem that Herr Doktor Pfnür had meant his promise of a grand tour in a painfully literal sense. Mab's brow wrinkled. It was odd that they should be shown every nook and cranny. Almost as if the Friendly Buzzard were saying, "Look, no skeletons in *my* closet." Unless, Bluebeard-like, he meant to show them behind every door but one. Not that he could really be holding Dr. Bird prisoner, but there might be some Guilty Secret. As Mab considered embroidering a story around this new idea, she determined to keep a lookout for the Unopened Door. She was about to warn Perry to do likewise when Doktor Pfnür turned.

Beaming mysteriously, like a magician about to perform some astonishing feat of legerdemain, Pfnür announced, "And now, my young friends, as you say in English, 'the last but not the least.' We come now to the heart of my little kingdom. It is off limits to our young men, even, for reasons you may soon guess." With a ghastly twinkle, he waved the children after Oriole into another old-fashioned cage of an elevator, slid the gate shut, and adjusted the control lever. Mab was just about to mouth silently to Perry, "*Do* you think he's trying to show us he hasn't got Daddy hidden away?" when Doktor Pfnür's stooped shoulders swiveled half around. As his long neck and thick spectacles craned down, the better to smile at her, Mab's

73

suspicious frown was whisked away in favor of a demure look of Suspenseful Interest. The elevator touched bottom with an audible bump.

In spite of their growing resistance to the heavy-handed geniality of the doctor's tourist-guide manner, the children were impressed by the cellars. Mab was entranced. Oriole made Perry writhe by crossing her hands over her heart and exclaiming, "Marvelous! How perfectly Gothic!" Herr Doktor Pfnür beamed and patted her on the shoulder.

The elevator itself had opened into a large rock-hewn, shelf-lined, disused pantry, while a wide archway to the right gave onto a much larger chamber lit by scores of electric candles in heavy wrought-iron wall sconces. Their glow on walls rough-hewn from the living rock gave the room and its heavy antique furniture the look of a real castle. An electric fire glowed in one corner, but nothing else was modern. There were wolfskin and sheepskin rugs, dozens of rolled maps upended in a handsome copper cauldron, and unrolled maps held flat on the long table by piles of old leatherbound books. Even the huge mastiff dozing by the empty fireplace might have just that moment sprung alive from the pages of a medieval storybook.

"It's the Necromancer's Den!" breathed Mab, her suspicions forgotten.

Doktor Pfnür laughed, perhaps a shade too heartily. "Indeed. All it lacks is the crystal ball and alchemist's crucible. But here is nothing so interesting, I fear. This is where I come to be away from the bustle of our hearty young men, perhaps to plan and write a talk to give to one of the many Alpine Clubs I visit in Germany and Italy, or to balance our monthly accounts. All very dull, you see." He moved across the room to open the heavy oaken door opposite.

"But here is my little treasure house." He beamed. "We must choose one of its gems as a farewell gift for your mother."

At the "farewell" the Birds exchanged glances, but prudently said nothing. As for the gem, whatever Mab and Perry had expected, they were disappointed. The treasure house was simply the Pfnürs' wine cellar. Planned to supply the ill-fated hotel, it had survived the sanitarium years unused but intact. Tall racks for bottles lined the rock-hewn walls, and at the room's farther end more racks stood in rows like library stacks. Doktor Pfnür moved along the nearest rack, giving each bottle a half turn as he checked the labels. "A Moselle, I think. 1964. 1961? Ah, here. A lovely, delicate wine." Drawing a white wine from its resting place, he tweaked out an enormous handkerchief and dusted the bottle lovingly. "A *Bernkasteler Doktor*. Incomparable bouquet. You must tell your mother, Fräulein Oriole, that there is not a meal to be had in Riesenmoos worthy of it. Such a wine should be saved until you are once more in Salzburg."

"She'll think that a hard condition." Oriole flashed her most winning smile, much to Mab's disgust. If Herr Doktor Pfnür had been fishing to find out whether the Birds were in the Eiswinkel for more than a day or two, he had baited his hook well. Oriole's gracious answer made it quite clear that Salzburg was more than a day or two in the offing. Oriole, oblivious of everything except what was an unusually elegant gift to send a perfect stranger, thanked their host profusely.

The doctor beamed with pleasure as he gently set the bottle on a small table in the center of the wine cellar and moved to usher the children before him into another, smaller room. "My Chamber of Horrors." He chuckled.

Perry's look of boredom returned almost as soon as it had vanished. The room was crammed with weather-worn sculptures: funereal vases of flowers in marble, larger-than-life-size Apollos, nymphs and satyrs, Roman statesmen, a Swan Knight, and a desperate-looking Valkyrie who gave the impression that her horse had been stolen while she wasn't looking. When Mab suggested as much, Pfnür gravely agreed.

"Yes, I have wondered at her distress since first we brought her down here. These, you see, were the garden ornaments. They are worthless copies, of course, but too amusing to break up into gravel even though they were not suitable for the Hochgebirgsschule. A good-humored conclusion to our little tour, *ja?*" Outside, he briefly opened a heavy iron door Mab had set her heart on for the Unopened Room, and a torrent of noise spilled out. "Here there are only the generator and furnaces. So! For our tea we shall return to the Necromancer's Den, as the little Fräulein calls it. My good Frau should be awaiting us there."

Not a single door unopened. As they retraced their steps, Mab was forced to admit to herself that, castle or no, the Pfnürs were too dreadfully dull to be truly Dreadful. Klara Pfnür, neat and businesslike in a gray suit and white polo-neck sweater, was at the dumb-waiter next to the elevator. Everything about her was quiet efficiency: the formal apologies for having been delayed; the speed with which the long table was cleared, the cloth spread, and a tempting array of jelly buns, almond-apricot cookies, *Tascherln*, cream-filled cupcakes, and *Faschingskrapfen* laid down the middle; and the precise level to which she poured the

76

tea in each cup. Everything about Frau Pfnür was, more-over, solid and colorless, except for the bright red spot that flamed on each cheek—and even those paled as she kept up her determinedly colorless chat.

When Oriole and the well-stuffed children escaped at last with the precious bottle and a small bag of pastries, they compared notes and agreed. They had learned nothing except one bit of news Frau Pfnür let fall in the course of describing her uneventful day: Byron Fleischacker, Herr Glöckner, and Father Sepp, the village priest, had been congratulating each other over wine and *Kugelhupf* in the Weinstube of the Hotel Gappenwirt. If Frau Pfnür wondered what Byron was up to, she managed to conceal her curiosity admirably. The small black eyes never brightened, her square, stubby hands lay lifeless in her lap, and her small, pale smile seemed pasted on. The children were glad to be gone.

"I wonder what old Byron *has* been up to? At least someone's had a good day," Perry grumbled after the Pfnürschule VW bus had deposited them at the bottom of the Strumpfs' steep road. He felt a familiar pang in his lower jaw, and though a tentative probe with his tongue met with no tenderness, he knew he was in for another siege of toothache.

Oriole, after the quickest change her mother had ever known her to make, was off to meet Byron for dinner and to hear his news. Perry's toothache had begun to pain him in earnest, throbbing fiercely for two or three seconds, easing off, and then starting up again. It left him in no mood for supper but, considering all the pastry he had put away at the Pfnürs', he was in little danger of starving before morning. Mrs. Bird produced aspirin and borrowed the Strumpfs' oil of cloves for the toothache, but nothing helped.

"If it isn't better by morning," Mrs. Bird said thoughtfully, "I think we will go into Salzburg. You ought to see a dentist." To Perry's protest that they ought not leave Riesenmoos, she answered, "I've begun to think that might be *just* what we have to do. These people seem bent on mystifying us at every turn. And I want to get up on that plateau. I've had a feeling all along that the answer is up there. What your Mr. Lanz told you makes me even more sure, even if he does insist that Jeffrey and Gus came right back down again. What *is* sure is that we're not going to be able to hire a guide in Riesenmoos. But if we moved on to Abtenau—"

"No, Mom, wait—" Perry, between pangs, described to his mother the odd little procession they had seen trudging up to the Eisriesenhöhle. "There's some far-out stuff going on here, and it's all got something to do with these Ice-Ghost whatsises. We can't just up and leave now . . . *ow!*"

Mrs. Bird clucked sympathetically as Perry winced and pointed to his jaw. "All right, dear. I'll go away and stop chattering at you. I do have some letters to write. If you don't feel like reading, why don't you see if you can get some music on your transistor." As she bent down to put the aspirin and oil of cloves bottles in the small cupboard in the nightstand, her eye was caught by a pale glimmering in the shadow under Mab's bed. Kneeling, she fished until her fingers touched the corner of a scrap of paper that had worked its way under the edge of the worn carpet. It was a *Trib* clipping about a dam breaking in a tiny valley in northern Italy, and the icy flood that resulted. Mrs. Bird, turning it over, stood for a minute lost in thought.

"Oh, and Perry? When Mab comes up, will you please tell her I'd like to see her in my room?"

Mab was busy plotting. Because she had not seen Hansl before or during the evening meal, she insisted on helping a haggard Frau Strumpf clear the dishes and cornered him in the kitchen. Kani Strumpf nodded to her from his chair beside the stove. He was whittling, with delicate, quick movements surprising for such large hands, a strange little figure of a running child—with a cow's head instead of a human one. Hansl sat at the other side of the fire, a small imitation of his father, working on an awkward but similar figure. Instead of a cow's head, Hansl's had a tiny face surrounded by what might have been petals or leaves.

"Hey, I saw figurines like that down at Metzgers'." Mab forgot for a moment the urgent business that had brought her to the kitchen. "Why do they have such strange heads?"

It was Hansl who answered with a shrug. "I do not know. In the wintertime everyone carves them, and in the spring Herr Metzger takes many to the *Heimatwerke* shop in Salzburg to be sold to the tourists."

"What do you call them?"

"Nothing. 'Riesenmoos work,' I suppose. They have no name even though they are very old." He pointed toward the shelf above the kitchen window, where four delicately painted figures about eight inches tall, barefooted, hand in hand, danced along: a slender boy with a bull's head, a cow-headed girl in a pretty dirndl, then a boy whose hair was a mass of shiny green leaves, and last a laughing little

79

girl with a face framed in a ring of yellow daisy petals. "My great-grandfather carved those," Hansl said proudly. "They are the best in the Eiswinkel."

They were lovely. For a minute the kitchen was quiet except for the clink of dishes and the *s-snick* of knives, but then Mab remembered why she was there. "I like the cow-headed one best, I think," she said. That much was true, but she went on to say innocently, "But then I'm crazy about cows. I mean, I've never met one, but I've always wanted to. Up close, that is, not from across a fence away off in a field."

Hansl's quizzical look was a little wary, but his father glanced up from his handiwork with mild amusement to say, "Once we had many cows. Now there is only Grissel. Hansl will make you known to Grissel, if you wish."

"Right now?"

"*Now?*" Hansl was incredulous.

"Yes, now." Mab went to get her coat before he could object.

Hansl closed the door from the kitchen and hung his lantern on a hook in the hall between kitchen and dairy. Several pairs of rubber boots stood in a row along the wall, and after pointing out a pair for Mab, Hansl pulled his own on over his shoes. "Those are Mama's," he said. "They will be too large for you, but they will not fall off. She will not allow you back in the house if your feet are mucky."

Mab obeyed meekly, but once into the barn with the door closed, she did not even wait for Hansl to hang the lamp on its bracket. "Grissel can wait," she said. "Right now you can tell me what all of you were doing up there at that cave at lunchtime."

Hansl started, then turned slowly. In the lamplight his thin, peaky face was as pale as his silver-blond hair. "You saw? How could you see? We made sure there was no one in the forest or on the slopes."

"We were across the valley. Gabriel had field glasses."

"Oh." The word was full of disappointment. "Then Gabriel will stop being my friend now. He says that you do not keep secrets from friends. But many times you *must*. I could not speak of it to an outsider. I *cannot*." The pleading note made it very clear that keeping silent was, for Hansl, very difficult.

"O.K., then. If that's the way you want it. I'll just go around telling everybody you've told me all sorts of interesting things. They'll believe it. People generally do. And then you'll figure you might as well tell me so as to get rid of us sooner. So why not tell me now? It'll save time."

Hansl stared at her helplessly. His resistance went no further than a half-hearted, "But that is—how do you say it?—'blackmail'."

Mab nodded cheerfully.

As Hansl reluctantly pieced the story together, Riesenmoos had once been a prosperous and pleasant village with perhaps a little more than its share of flowers, fair weather, and healthy children. When the Pfnürs first came, their gift of the new drag lift had attracted just enough skiers in the wintertime to bring the village a little extra money and no inconvenience. Four years ago—a very deep, hard winter, Hansl recalled—Julius Bischof had climbed the ridge and lost himself in a blizzard on the plateau. Julius

Bischof was the best mountaineer in the district. Oh, he had found himself again and staggered into one of the climbers' huts on the Königskogel. Mountain Rescue searchers had found him there, badly frostbitten and insisting —as he continued to insist all the way to the hospital—that he had seen ghosts. "Aye, one of the old Ice Ghosts, like the old pictures in the church. Tall as a tree, it was, and moaning very fierce. I could not see well, for the snow, but when I cried out it gave a sort of shriek and shriveled away to nothing. Saint Martin be my witness, but it did."

At first no one but the children had listened. Their parents would not take it seriously even when the valley's good fortune began to sour. The first winter it was little things, little patches of bad luck: bread that would not rise, cakes that fell in the oven, the poor radio reception that grew steadily worse. The deeper changes grew more slowly, until winter in the Eiswinkel meant sleeplessness and short tempers, fretful babies, barking dogs, and skittish cattle. But by that time a young climber from the Hochgebirgsschule and Schoolmistress Muhlbach, who was fond of moonlit walks, had seen the ghosts. Something had disturbed Them. Something had set Them walking after hundreds of years of peace.

The Eiswinkel was cursed. Riesenmoosers drew in upon themselves, and in the deepest part of winter even Doktor Pfnür (who steadfastly denied that such things as ghosts could exist) gave the Pfnürschule trainees a long holiday. Being outsiders, they could not be expected to stay.

By the time old Herr Glöckner remembered about the Ice Brides and the offerings that had saved later village maidens from a like fate, the Riesenmoosers were ready to try anything. For a while it seemed to have worked. At least the ghost-giants disappeared after Carnival was over; but the valley had barely begun to recover when November loomed again. Each year come Carnival the villagers sent the children with their gifts of bread and salt and herbs up to the great wrought-iron gates that had closed off the Eisschemenhöhle for as long as anyone could remember. Each year the result was the same: on Ash Wednesday the troubles began to dwindle, and woodcutters and climbers could go out on the mountain and have no ghost-giants warn them away.

"It sounds just like the Dark Ages, or whatever." Mab pushed away a small brown goat intent upon eating her sleeve buttons. "Byron—he's this friend of my sister's—Byron says Carnival was really to chase the winter demons away, not to have One Last Orgy before Lent."

"Orgy?" Hansl shook his head. "I do not know the word."

"Well, I *think* it means you eat so much and drink so much that you feel kind of ogre-ish. I'm not sure."

"What is it, an ogre?"

"It's—" The problems of distinguishing an ogre from, say, an Ice Ghost were too complicated. "It's not important," Mab said impatiently. "What's important is that all that demon-stuff can't be any realer now than it was then. It's just a figment in everybody's head." She rubbed her own forehead as if it ached a little. "Just because somebody mistakes a tree for a giant in a snowstorm, everybody else starts seeing giants."

"No, it is not like that at all." Hansl's earlier reluctance to talk was forgotten. He paced up and down the straw-covered floor nervously. "You feel it yourself. And I have seen the tracks of the ghost that lives on the Königskogel.

It lurks sometimes in the wood above the Riesenalm. Twice it has frighted Mama."

This year, Hansl explained, had been worse than ever. The old women moaned that this year the ghosts would not leave at all, because of what had happened last year at Carnival. For as long as anyone could remember there had been at Carnival time only a short religious procession on Shrove Tuesday, but last year Father Sepp and Fräulein Muhlbach proposed making it a real celebration. Fräulein Muhlbach thought it would cheer the village to mark the passing of winter. After the gifts were taken to the Eisschemenhöhle on the Monday, there should be a general merrymaking, and on Tuesday an old-fashioned Carnival procession and a great feast before the midnight Mass to mark the beginning of Lent. Had Mab seen the six carved gargoyle faces on the ceiling of the church? It had been thought that they were a part of the beams they decorated, but Father Sepp discovered that they were masks, hanging there from the long forgotten days when the village elders wore them on tall frameworks and played Ice Ghosts in the old play. With new frames and flowing white robes, they had made truly frightening giants. "Just like the real thing," Fräulein Muhlbach had faltered, losing a little of her enthusiasm.

On the day of the procession, all had gone well despite a steady snowfall. Starting at the Mooserkreuz cross, the swaying giants danced their stately, lumbering sword dance; and once in the village streets they knocked on certain doors, roaring threats that brought out the other masked dancers: the fool, the butcher, a floury baker, a tipsy tinker, and a gossipy old crone. These the giants drove ahead of them until midway through the village,

84

where the following crowd was supposed to take heart and chase the ghosts of winter on down the Moosweg. Were supposed to. But then a bystander counted nine giants in the swirling snow . . . nine ghosts where there should have been six. Word spread like grassfire, and the villagers fled in all directions. A nervous Father Sepp, two altar boys, and the tiny choir were left to straggle on in terror to the end of the snowy town. There they found their own six giants, unmasked and faint with fright, and no trace of the others.

An evil omen. But worse was to come. On the last day of summer the garland of flowers that was, according to custom, thrown into the Riesenbach with prayers for summer's return, had not floated down the stream, but sank instead like a stone. What could be expected but the worst? And the worst came. This winter had been the harshest in memory, with deepening poverty and much sickness.

"For this, you must see why so many folk wish you gone. They fear that your poking and prying will anger the ghosts again and bring even worse fortune upon the Eiswinkel."

"Again? You mean like Daddy's poking around up there in the mountains? Oh, come off it! You can't keep pretending you don't know anything about that, Hansl Strumpf. Gabriel saw him. Twice, with Professor Bachner." She fixed him with an accusing eye. "All that talk about asking your friends, and how exciting the detecting would be . . . You never *meant* to help us find where Daddy went."

Hansl would not meet her eyes. "Perhaps they were in Riesenmoos after all. Here at Haus Strumpf we do not know all that happens in the village. We are—how you say?—issolated."

"Isolated," Mab corrected absently, scratching the little goat's bony skull. When she stopped, it nudged her hand insistently. "It's no good all of you telling us to go away," she said fretfully. "Not until the plateau's searched, and all those caves. Even if nobody helps, Mama says now that we know the way they went, we can call in Mountain Rescue people from outside." A quick glance told her that this was a new thought to Hansl. The Riesenmoosers must not know that Abtenau's local Mountain Rescue team had already searched the area above the Tricklfall trail and declared further search useless.

"Gabriel would not guide you?" Hansl rubbed his forehead.

"No. He says 'Go away home' too. But nobody gives us a real reason. Even—even if it's true about your old giants, w-why should we go?" Mab was half crying, her palms pressed to her temples. The little goat bleated and butted his head again and again against the feed bin she sat on.

"A reason?" The word seemed suddenly to anger Hansl. Grabbing Mab's arms, he shook her like a limp rag doll. "It is reasons you want, but I have gived them and you do not listen. Listen to the singing in your head. It is a reason, *ja?* Look how the little goat beats on herself—she is a reason. You do not believe this has to do with the *Eisschemen?* Very good. You wish reasons: come, I will show you one you cannot reason away."

Hansl dragged Mab after him into the dark, narrow hallway. At the end away from the kitchen door, beyond the boots and coats, he reached something down from a high shelf, and then very quietly eased the upper half of the double door open onto the winter night. "I have oiled the hinges," he whispered. "Every night I watch from this place. Here, take this. I will point it for you where to look.

"It" was a cardboard tube about ten inches long, and though it was not like Gabriel's field glasses, the tube cut out the glare of bright moonlight on the steep, snowy Riesenalm and focused Mab's squint upward where Hansl guided it. "Move it back and forth. Along the edge of the forest. You will see. It comes because of you people. Until your—until you are here it never came in moonlight, or so close. It had went away. But now that you are come, it is always here again."

At first there was nothing, only the steep, silvered slope of the high field, with the great forest above stooping down to lap at its edge. After a moment, Mab could make out dark tree trunks and low sweeping branches gray against the blackness. Nothing else. Nothing until, incredibly, it seemed one tall trunk separated itself from another, wavered to the edge of the moon-filled field, grew pale, and then distinct. Tall and unbending, it swayed gently as a tree does, but it was no tree. Spiky locks, icicle-like, shadowed a face whose eyes were, Mab knew, watching, searching.

seven

" 'Morning, Mab dear." Mrs. Bird hastily swallowed
the last bite of her slice of toast. "I'm glad you're down
early. When I came in from using the phone down at the
Gappenwirt last night, you were already asleep. It took
great strength of character not to drag you bodily out of
bed. Here, look at this." She drew the clipping from under
her plate and handed it across the table. "Do you know
anything about this?"

Under a headline of *Disaster Might Be Cheaper*, the
short article reported that after widespread avalanches in
the western Italian Alps and the Dolomites had caused
minor flooding along the Oglio and Adige Rivers and in
the towns along Lake Como and Lake Garda, indus-
trialists in Brescia, Verona, and Vicenza had taken out
flood insurance with the Fairweather Insurance Group of
Hartford, Connecticut. Fairweather's Rome representative
declined to quote their premium rates or reveal the names
of their clients, but reports were that the single-premium

rates ran into six figures—in dollars, not lire.

"Gosh! Wouldn't a company have to be loaded to afford that?"

Mrs. Bird waved an impatient hand. "I don't know. Perhaps a number of them go together. Something like a Chamber of Commerce might be able to afford it. But that's not important. What do you know about the clipping itself? Is it yours or one of Daddy's?"

"It's not mine. First time I've seen it. Only, I didn't read all of Daddy's. It might be one of them." Mab turned it over. A portion of a column of New York Stock Exchange quotations read at the top —*ry 1, 1972 Closing Prices.* "It's Daddy's, I guess. I didn't start cutting things like this out until you told us about his. But . . . January first or February first?" Her head raised slowly as it dawned on her. "But Daddy left home *before* New Year's."

Her mother snatched it back. "Good Lord! Then it must be—" She compared the article with the front page of the Paris edition of the *Herald-Tribune* she had collected on her trip into the village. "The type face *is* the same. All the ones in your father's file are from the New York or L.A. *Times* or the Pasadena *Star-News.* And if this is at least three and a half weeks old. . . ."

"*Where did you find it?*" gasped Oriole. She and Perry had arrived unnoticed.

"Under Mabbit's bed."

"You mean Pop and Dr. Bachner stayed *here?*" Perry was bewildered. "That doesn't make any sense. Why would the Strumpfs lie about it?"

"Well, to be fair, dear, they may not have. We asked a lot of people if they'd seen your father or Gus Bachner, but come to think of it, I never did ask the Strumpfs. I suspect that Elisabeth—and perhaps Kani—are as superstitious as the rest of Riesenmoos, if not more so. Everyone seems utterly terrified of having things—meaning their Ghosts, I take it—stirred up. I suppose we must have looked easy enough to pacify."

"Maybe *they* didn't lie, but that Hansl did." Mab was furious. "Him and his, 'We don't know everything that goes on in the village because we are so issolated!'" She paused abruptly. Hansl had said something else, something about the ghosts not appearing on moonlit nights "until you're . . ." Then he had corrected it to "until you are here." *But it had been "your," not "you're."* He had been about to say "your father." Mab wondered if he hadn't wanted to tell her but had, like everyone else, been too frightened.

"What is it, Mab?"

"Oh, nothing." They wouldn't believe her if she told about the ghost. Oriole would be sure it was just another wild tale. Now, in broad daylight, Mab wasn't sure she believed it herself. She trickled cream in careful patterns over her oatmeal. "I guess Mama's right. They're all just too scared. Except Gabriel, maybe."

"Oriole?" Mrs. Bird eyed her elder daughter thoughtfully. "Do you think that young man might be persuaded to guide you and me up to those caves and over the ridge?"

"No." Oriole flushed. "I asked last night, and he said no. Flat out. Not even an explanation, and he'd been very sweet up to then." She blushed. "So I—um, batted my eyelashes delicately and asked 'pretty please.'"

"And?" Mrs. Bird did not ask what Byron had been doing during all this. It was clear that at some point he had dropped out of Oriole's evening.

Oriole slumped back in her chair with a look of sulky bafflement. "He laughed and said I'd get up on the plateau over his dead body. And then he had the nerve to ask if I was wearing false eyelashes."

"Maybe he's in on it," said Perry darkly.

Oriole bridled. "They're my *own* eyelashes."

"Eyelashes? Who cares about your eyelashes? I mean, maybe he's in on the *plot*. Something's going on, and we know it isn't ghosts. First off, Dad may have been onto something. Remember, Mom said he thought there was something fishy about all the earthquakes and avalanches over here this winter."

" 'Unnatural,' " Mrs. Bird corrected mildly. " 'A very unnatural disturbance pattern,' he said."

"Meaning what, exactly?" Oriole waggled a cautionary spoon. "For all we know, Daddy could have meant simply 'unusual' or 'puzzling.' If you want to know what *I* think, I think all this local superstition has warped everyone's judgment. You're thinking that '*un*natural' means '*super*natural.' " She eyed her mother with particular distrust, remembering the ouija board.

"My dear, I believe in neither ghosts nor demons." Mrs. Bird buttered another roll. "There *is* another possibility: 'man-made.' "

"Oh, *Mama!* That's as absurd as saying that the Demons of Winter have been acting up."

"O.K., O.K.," placated Perry. "We don't know *what* he meant. But just for a minute suppose he didn't have an accident, and that he isn't up there trapped in a cave drinking melted ice water and eating his shoelaces."

Oriole shuddered, and even Mab, paling, lowered her spoonful of sugared cereal and tipped it back into her bowl.

Mrs. Bird stared through the parlor wall as if she were already miles away, probing the mountain's innards.

Perry went on doggedly. "If he isn't, then it could be that there is something afoot, and somebody has him. Orry can go on looking as if she sat on a tack, but it won't make some of the things that have been going on around here look any less queer. You know that toothache of mine? Well, last night, late, I tried to get the Armed Forces Network on my transistor to find out what the basketball scores were and how UCLA was doing. I knew it would be fuzzy—Gabriel's right about the lousy reception—but at night it's usually better, and that's a pretty good little radio. O.K.? Then listen: just after I found the AFN—they broadcast out of some U. S. Army base in Germany—it got creamed out by a really weird blast of static. Anyhow, that's what I thought it was at first. The interference was so bad I was afraid my eyes were going to pop out before I could get the dumb earphone out of my ear. It kept coming at two-second intervals: two on and two off. You could hear the same pulse on all the high frequencies, but at that one spot it was really fierce."

Oriole shifted impatiently, but Mrs. Bird was clearly caught.

"And—" said Mab, impatiently.

"*And my tooth was doing the same thing*. Two on and two off. Every once in a while there'd be a longish wait, and then it would start up again. Whatever it is, it's powerful, and not far from here. A secret radio station. High-frequency coded stuff, maybe."

"Such melodrama!" Oriole managed a look of kindly amusement. "*And* from a radio expert. Perry, everyone's heard tales of people receiving radio broadcasts on dental fillings. It's quirky, but perfectly natural. There's no need to embroider mysterious plots around it. That's more Mab's style. Well, it *is*, Mama," she protested as Mrs. Bird raised an eyebrow. "The next thing we know, he'll have it that we've stumbled onto a—a Communist spy network," she sputtered, half indignant, half laughing. "One that abducts Western scientists, spiriting them behind the Iron Curtain through a string of caves that goes all the way to the Hungarian border."

Mrs. Bird considered this for a moment and then said with a seriousness that made Oriole sigh, "No-o. I hardly think that's likely. But I'd like to know why Perry says a 'secret' radio station."

Perry shrugged. "No real reason. I can't think why they would be sending a slow pulse like that at long irregular intervals. Voices or scrambled voices or something with a recognizable code pattern—that's what you usually get. Besides, this is some kind of speeded-up super high frequency. It's such a narrow band that practically all you have to do is breathe on the radio and you lose it and have to fiddle to get it back. That close to the AFN frequency, it's just a blip you'd normally tune right past to bring the AFN in clearer. Doesn't that seem like somebody wants to make sure it isn't noticed?"

"Perhaps." Mrs. Bird sighed. "Though I don't see what connection it can have with Jeffrey. Everything gets curiouser and curiouser. I can't think of a thing more we can do at this point. I should have brought my needlepoint with me. It would be wonderfully reassuring to be working at something with a nice, clear pattern." She folded her napkin. "I'll have to muddle all this over on my way down to the Gappenwirt. I have to check whether there's any answer yet to the cablegram I sent Skinny Esterbrook. I thought he might know something about that Seismological Forecasting Service."

"Wait for me, will you, Mama? I'll walk down with you," said Oriole, pitching into her breakfast. "I think I'll go in to early Mass."

"I might as well come along too," said Perry, "and see if old Byron's out of the sack yet. If he's not off to church with you, that is."

"Byron?" Oriole gave a discontented little snort. "For all I know he's been there all night, translating his old medieval manuscript. He was so full of it at dinner last night that I didn't hear a word about anything else. When your friend Gabriel showed up, dear Mr. Fleischacker turned me and his dessert over to him and went trotting back to his grubby little muniments room, or whatever they call the church library." She made a little *moue* of disgust and then turned back to eye her brother curiously. "What do you want to find him for?"

"Nothing much," Perry evaded. "I just thought I'd see how he was coming along."

Mab climbed the stairs slowly. If only Perry were right, and there turned out to be a neat scientific explanation for even a tiny slice of the Eiswinkel's mystery! But how did you manage scientifically to explain away a ten-foot-tall giant? Fairy tales, Mab decided regretfully, were more comfortable in print than in person. Giants didn't bear much thinking about. Think about something else. What was it her mother had said? Something about patterns. About having nice, clear patterns to work from . . .

"A pattern!" Mab halted in the middle of the upstairs

94

hall. Somewhere in that sheaf of her father's clippings there might be a pattern. There had to be. Of course, only an expert would know what was odd about any one of the events described, but if all together they fell into some sort of pattern, it might give a clue to what had struck Professor Bird as worth poking into. Mab gathered her own clippings from an assortment of pockets and, slipping into the room Mrs. Bird shared with Oriole, locked the door and opened the suitcase that stood on the luggage rack. The large manila envelope lay on top.

There were thirty-five clippings in all, the large map, and several computer print-out sheets with lists of dates, latitude and longitude readings, and numbers that might have been seismographical measurements. Mab propped the map against a pillow, spread the newspaper cuttings out below it on the spread, and then sat herself cross-legged at the bottom of the bed to contemplate the mystery. Nothing. Staring at them compellingly didn't help either. Something for a moment teetered on the edge of falling into place, but teetered right back again. Earthquakes of all sizes. Avalanches. Floods. All of them scattered in and around the Swiss, Austrian, German, Italian, and Yugoslavian Alps. At least most of the clippings were dated, either in her father's blue-pencil scrawl or in her own tidy Bic-pen script. Otherwise, the puzzle would have been utterly hopeless.

There was, of course, the ouija board, lurking beneath Mrs. Bird's sweaters and socks. She might give each clipping a number and see what pattern ouija traced out on the board, but Mab didn't think her subconscious was quite up to that.

"By date. That's the most obvious way to classify clippings." She shuffled through and rearranged them as if they were playing cards, and came up with four from the previous winter and two larger and almost equally divided groups, covering this winter from the past October to New Year's and from mid-January on. No one of the three groupings gave any hint of rhyme or reason. At first glance the four earliest disturbances could not have been more various: a low-scale sustained tremor at Graz, in the Austrian province of Styria, had caused only minor structural damage and a temporary radio blackout; near Garmisch, the fashionable Bavarian resort, a highly localized tremor had jarred the Zugspitze, Germany's highest mountain, triggering a power blackout that had marooned cog-railway cars and pedestrians in the mountain tunnels for two hours; and in the mountains above St. Leonhard in Italy, there had been a serious avalanche despite a sudden cold snap. Later, without the excuse of an early thaw, widespread slides north of Belluno had caused flooding along the River Piave.

Dividing the clippings according to kinds of disturbances produced a similar blank. Not even pulling her eyes into slits with a finger at the corner of each eye—one of Mab's most reliable Aids to Concentration—could make the collection of disasters blur into a meaningful whole. She sat back on her heels and scowled. The sense that there *was* a pattern was stronger than ever, but the pattern itself was as elusive as quicksilver is to the touch. Ouija, behind her in the suitcase at the foot of the bed, began to be tempting.

As Mab slid off the bed the map bent over on its center fold and collapsed on the pillow. The map! "How dumb can you get? No, don't answer that," Mab cautioned the bedpost. Fetching her colored sketching pencils from the adjoining room, she spread the map out flat and marked Graz, Garmisch, St. Leonhard, and Belluno in blue. They were all about the same distance from Riesenmoos but, apart from that, suggested nothing. The clippings from the November and December just past gave a much more interesting spatter of dots on the map. Mab marked the rash of avalanches in red: a spot forty kilometers east of St. Moritz, and others in Italy—in the Alpi Orobie, the Adamello, the Gruppo di Brenta, and the Dolomites. Temperatures had been rising at the time, and the result had been minor floods along the rivers Oglio and Adige and around Lake Como and Lake Garda. Mab shaded the affected towns with slightly larger red dots; and again with smaller ones, she marked the two moderate quakes that had centered near Ptuj and Krško in Yugoslavia. She sat back and scowled. There were clusters, to be sure—Italian Alps, nearby Italian lakes and rivers—but what was unnatural about that?

It was the green pencil that did it. The third batch of clippings included floods in Monza and Padua, an earthquake in Zagreb, and another rash of avalanches: in the Vorarlberg in Austria, in Liechtenstein, and in the Graubünden and Albula Alps, from which the runoff had dangerously raised the level of Lake Constance. Last and least was a tiny prick of green by the dot that stood for Munich, where a freakish tremor had destroyed the Hohenzollern Bridge over the Isar and a large granite obelisk in the nearby Englischer Garten without doing any damage at all to the garden's Chinese tower, or to the Max Joseph or J. F. Kennedy bridges, both close by.

"It's there . . . It's there . . ." Mab rocked back and forth, squinting fiercely. It was like trying to thread through a maze when there was nothing to go on but a dimly felt awareness that somewhere ahead a door is open and a breeze

97

stirs. At last, wetting the red pencil on her tongue, Mab measured her forefinger against the scale at the bottom of the map and marked off forty kilometers. Then with the finger as a ruler, she measured the first winter's four disturbances. All four were approximately 160 kilometers from the Tennen-Gebirge and Riesenmoos. This winter's were all between 160 and 240 kilometers from the same center. More than that, there seemed to be a crazy sort of purpose in the choice of locations. If the first four were isolated and dissimilar—almost a sampling of Available Disturbances—in contrast, late November's avalanches had spread methodically across the Italian Alps, touching off December's floods *only in rivers and lakes that could threaten sizeable cities:* Monza, Brescia, Verona, Vicenza, and Padua. And while Brescia, Verona, and Vicenza had at some time in January bought flood insurance from Fairweather and apparently stayed high and dry, Monza and Padua had just this week been flooded.

"Mavis Bird, you may be losing your marbles," Mab cautioned herself. "That's saying somebody's managing the weather, and that's impossible." But . . . there was that odd Seismological Forecasting story. If they had a service cities could subscribe to, then Ravenna surely would after its near-miss. But no one could prevent earthquakes. The best you could hope for was a warning. Ptuj and Krško had been Zagreb's warning, in a way. But how could you be sure what you thought was a warning wasn't a threat? Suppose—suppose you were a city and after your warning you were told that you must subscribe (or take out insurance) Or Else?

"But that's *crazy.*"

All the same, Mab took another look at the map. Say she wasn't completely crack-brained, and the whole idea wasn't beyond belief: then the slides in the western Alps that swelled the Upper Rhine and Lake Constance must be a threat aimed somewhere else. Where else but on down the Rhine? The river ran north off the map, but Mab remembered something of it from a Social Studies report she had done (written, Mab-fashion, from the point of view of a log that floated down from the mountains and, after numerous edifying adventures, ended up as wooden clogs in Holland). In the lowlands where flood dangers were the greatest, the Rhine flows through one of Europe's richest industrial areas. Cologne and Düsseldorf could be brought to a standstill by a major flood. They were perfect blackmail targets: rich and vulnerable. But the obelisk and bridge in Munich were a puzzle. They seemed too piddling as disasters to be part of a megalomaniac plot, and yet theirs were the most unnatural disturbances of all.

"Arghh! My brain is full of bread crumbs!" Mab tossed the clippings in the air in disgust, and they came fluttering down around her like oversize confetti. She wondered what Perry would think of it all. She might tell him, but certainly not Oriole, and not their mother. If Molly was to try to bring the authorities in to investigate the Riesenmoosers' concealment of Professor Bird's whereabouts, the simpler the story, the better. Unless, of course, Professor Esterbrook cabled that Seismological Forecasting was decidedly fishy. Suddenly full of energy, Mab shot into the other bedroom to bundle up for out-of-doors.

On the front door-step Mab met a red-nosed, red-cheeked

and breathless Mrs. Bird and Perry. "I was just coming down to find you. Did the telegram come? What did it say?"

Mrs. Bird was already halfway up the stairs. Pausing in flight, she stuffed her gloves into a deep pocket and fumbled in her shoulder bag for a crumpled piece of paper, which she tossed down to Mab. "It didn't come. But read that. I have to hurry and pack a few things and be at Metzgers' shop in twenty minutes."

"Where are we going?" Mab hurried up the stairs after her and into the bedroom.

"Not you. Me. Read the letter." Mrs. Bird snatched a blouse and a pair of stockings from the makeshift clothesline above the bedroom sink, and stuffed them into the smaller of her suitcases, scooping up toothbrush and perfume in passing.

Mab read. *Bird, Hotel Gappenwirt, Riesenmoos. Dear Madame, I am gratified to inform you that Herr Doktor Bachner has regained lucidity and expresses the most strong desire to speak with you at the earliest possible. Yours most faithfully, Erich Leitner, Direktor, The Institut Sigmundhaus, Franzgasse 40, Vienna.* She looked up. "Does 'regained lucidity' mean Dr. Bachner remembers what happened to him?"

"I certainly hope so." Mrs. Bird snapped the case shut, settled her hat back on, and brushed past Perry—who had mounted the stairs at his usual leisurely pace. "Come along, both of you," she called after her. "We have to find Oriole, and the Metzgers are leaving as soon as eleven o'clock Mass is over. They go to their daughter's in Pfarr-Werfen for Sunday lunch and have offered to get me to the train. If we miss them, I won't have a way out until tomorrow."

Despite the difficulties of hurrying on icy, rutted roads, of finding Oriole to explain about Dr. Bachner, and of quieting her doubts about the wisdom of Acting in Haste, Mrs. Bird, the Metzgers, and the Metzgers' blue VW bus chugged out of sight down the tree-lapped road promptly at noon.

"I still say that if you act in haste you repent at leisure," Oriole maintained, in what Perry called her "first-grade-teacher voice." However, allowing for Oriole's being Oriole, her concern was not entirely misplaced. In the rush of the departure, Mrs. Bird went off without retrieving from Mab the note bearing Dr. Leitner's name and the clinic's address; and Perry had omitted to hand his mother's suitcase into the departing VW. Byron, trotting out of the Gappenwirt at 12:01 to say good-by, found all in confusion. "I thought you were all going," he said in some bewilderment. "The manager said you'd been called away."

Frantic explanations were drowned in a prodigious jangle of bells as Herr Glöckner drove around the corner from the church in a gaily painted sleigh drawn by a very shaggy small horse. "*Deus ex machina!*" exclaimed Byron, signaling Herr Glöckner to stop. "Enter stage right: the God in the Machine."

"Come on, we can't catch them in *that*," Perry protested.

Herr Glöckner, when the problem had been explained to him, disagreed and urged the children to crowd themselves and the unfortunate suitcase in the best way they could. The Metzgers, it seemed, always made a stop two miles down the road for their younger daughter, Lise, and her woodcutter husband. To overtake the Volkswagen at Lise's house would be of no difficulty. Herr Glöckner enjoyed a bit of a race, and Gretel, the little mare, had been itching for a downhill run. In a moment the last of the churchgoers coming along the Moosweg saw the Birds and Byron disappear in a snowy rush.

Perry's ride was the wildest. He rode perched on the high driver's seat beside Herr Glöckner, but the old gentleman at least had the long brake lever to steady himself against. With the steepness of the road, he had to pull on it very hard indeed to prevent the sleigh's running Gretel down. The little horse's ears were back, the whites of her eyes rolled, and for all that she looked like a round, hairy barrel, she galloped as if her life depended on it. Which it probably did. She reached the woodcutter's cottage in an astonishing five minutes, just as the little blue bus was loading its last passenger.

Mrs. Bird greeted her suitcase with surprise—as Oriole later sighed, she would not have missed it before bedtime in Vienna—and then with a cheerful beeping and much waving at the windows, the bus set off down the mountain.

Herr Glöckner, in a great good humor, pulled out a flask of apple brandy and offered it around while Gretel caught her breath. Perry would have taken it after Byron, but at a glare from Oriole returned it meekly. When at last Gretel's nervous quivering (and what Mab, predictably, referred to as the "tintinnabulation of her bells") had died down, Herr Glöckner and his crew climbed aboard for the trip back. On the steep bits the young people walked to lighten Gretel's load, and as they walked, they sang. After *Ho, Young Rider*, Herr Glöckner joined in with a sentimental rendition of *Mein Riesenmoos*. The only songs the Birds knew in German were *Stille Nacht, Heilige Nacht* and *O Tannenbaum*, and if they were a little late for Christmas, they seemed just right among the climbing, snow-clad pines. It was a long hill.

Once over the crest into Riesenmoos, winded, laughing, and red-cheeked, Byron, Oriole, and the children parted company with Gretel and her master at the Gappenwirt's front steps. Their entrance into that establishment's dining room in a cheerful rush of laughter and chatter was met by an uncomfortable silence. Not a fork clinked against a plate.

"Er—for four, please," Byron said to the waitress. The words fell into the sudden hush and rattled around the room like so many marbles.

Gabriel Lanz, eating alone, looked up from his *Paprika Schnitzel*, an angry flush on his pleasant face and a coldness in his eyes that was distinctly unpleasant. At the far corner table Herr Doktor Waldemar Pfnür and Frau Doktor Pfnür were frozen in surprise, mouths full, forks in mid-air. For a flickering instant, Frau Pfnür's beady black eyes glittered alarmingly, but a moment later were dull as ever under their drooping eyelids. The doctor had folded back into his usual stoop. Several other diners cleared their throats uncomfortably or coughed. The dining room seemed almost to quiver. Even the central heating rumbled unhappily.

"They thought we'd all gone, didn't they?" whispered Mab.

Oriole nodded and sat down with her back to Gabriel. For what may have been the first time in her life, she did not feel like saying a word.

eight

PERRY TILTED BACK IN HIS CHAIR, CRANING TO CATCH THE excited conversation at the table behind him, where the waitress chattered on at a great rate to the accompaniment of shocked noises from the diners.

"Did she say 'avalanche'?" asked Mab in a whisper as the girl moved on to the table beyond.

The word "avalanche" served as nothing else had to rouse Oriole from the morose silence she had slipped into. It even broke into Byron's preoccupation with an excellent dish of beefsteak and onions seasoned with caraway seeds. "Avalanche? Where? When was this?"

Perry leaned forward over his plate to whisper, "About a mile down the road to Werfenweng. About twenty minutes or so ago, just after we got back up. I didn't catch it all, but I think she said the road's blocked."

Oriole stared, for a moment uncomprehending. "Straighten up," she said absently. "You're getting gravy on your sweater." Behind the look of blank surprise, she was all confusion and alarm. It would not do to frighten the children. Keep calm. Where was Gabriel Lanz now? Oriole glanced around the room casually. Gone. Good. She took a deep breath and, without thinking, a large sip of Byron's wine. All that friendly interest, all that pretended concern . . . Mister Lanz's look of shock twenty minutes ago made it perfectly clear where he really stood. And how could so convenient an avalanche be an accident? Either the Birds were all supposed to be en route to Vienna, with the road closed behind them, or—Oriole shivered—closed *over* them. But that sort of thing only happened in television movies. Didn't it? She was imagining things. Sinister plots, indeed! But even with common sense restored, Oriole had a dreadful—and for Oriole, rare—sinking feeling that she did not know What to Do. Organization, as she always insisted, depends on a Plan, but plans depend on knowing what your problem is. She sighed helplessly, startling the others, who were whispering excitedly together. "Mama is going to be dreadfully worried when she hears," she said lamely.

"She's going to be more than that. *They* set it off. You know they did," Mab hissed. "Whoever runs that radio station of Perry's has something big going on up on the plateau, and they're afraid we'll find it. A—a something that can set off avalanches any old where, and make floods on the Rhine, and—"

"Radio station? What radio station?" Byron looked from Bird to Bird, lost.

"I'll tell you about it later," Perry said hastily. "There's something I wanted to ask about your tape recorder, too. It can wait until then."

Mab wished she had held her tongue. Oriole was rattled

enough, and Byron wasn't likely to be an ounce of help. Too polite to pry and having little curiosity about matters not folklorical, he resorted discreetly to a second helping of steak. Avoiding her sister's eyes, Mab followed suit, attacking her peas with unlikely enthusiasm. But evasion served only to delay explanations until the end of the main course. By the time dessert was on the table, Oriole had wrung from Mab an account of the clippings and the map and—it was like Oriole—had cheered up at having something concrete to disbelieve.

"It all sounds perfectly mad to me." Oriole swept through the swinging door with such energy that its rebound very nearly swept Mab back into the dining room. "Weather control. Flood blackmail. Fairy tales again, Mab! How is it done, pray tell? Tell me that."

"*Orry!* You don't have to *broadcast* it." At least the swinging door had stopped flapping, and the Pfnürs, lingering over their coffee, might not have heard. "Just forget it, will you?" Mab tied her hood. "I'll—I'll see you all later. I have to ask Hansl Strumpf about something."

Byron, having paid the bill, was counting the change from the Birds' share into Oriole's palm. He looked up. "You haven't seen all of the church yet, have you, Mab? It's worth taking a look at the paintings in the bell tower if you have a moment. They give a much clearer idea of what the *Eisschemen* must have looked like than what you can see from the old masks up on the chancel ceiling." He gave her an irritating Big-Brotherly smile. "Perhaps tomorrow, if not now."

Mab was half tempted to say that she knew exactly what they looked like, thank you; but she had to save that for when she could get Perry alone. Oriole would pronounce her hysterical and take to watching her like a worried mother cat. That would spoil everything.

Byron, had he been the one to see an Ice Ghost, would probably have cleared his throat and asked it to explain into the tape recorder what it had been doing since the Middle Ages. "I expect Oriole's told you," he went on with single-minded enthusiasm. "Miss Muhlbach and the ladies' guild are working hard to finish the new costumes. You'll be seeing the *real* ending of the Riesenmoos carnival play. The one that hasn't been played in five hundred years. Redis-covered characters, great action . . ." Wistfully he added, "Too bad about the road being closed. It's going to be the kind of thing *Life* or *Time* might cover."

"It's nice we'll be here for it," said Oriole, not very enthusiastically. She peered nervously out the front door.

"Yes, nice," agreed Mab, impatient to be out and away. How could anyone care about plays and paintings when there were *real* things to worry about? Somehow she had to wrangle Hansl Strumpf into taking her up to the Eissche-menhöhle. It was not going to be easy.

"Please? Fräulein Bird, if I could speak with you one moment?"

Gabriel Lanz had appeared out of the phone booth in the corner of the lobby, and Oriole could not have looked more alarmed had the phone booth been a bottle and Gabriel the unwelcome and evil genie. Byron—busy winding his muffler around his neck in a scientific manner—scarcely noticed as she was whisked unwillingly into a corner. The children watched mistrustfully, Mab deciding with regret that Ga-briel was a Something in Disguise, but a something not exactly pleasant. At the moment he looked decidedly unfriendly. Even the Pfnürs had managed not to scowl so blackly, and Mab had felt uneasy about Dr. Pfnür from the first. Perry, for his part, suspected that somewhere behind Frau Pfnür's bland imitation of a pudding lurked another Frau Pfnür, perhaps that dragon-for-discipline Gabriel had hinted at. Now that he thought of it, Gabriel's remark had been a very neat explanation of young Herr Friml's alarm at being seen with Oriole, but hardly the whole truth. Herr Friml had been, Perry guessed, "off limits." The few trainees he had seen in the village had been on specific errands. It did not make sense that they would *choose* to spend their free time at the school, but apparently they did. Curious. And Gabriel was curiouser. Like a friendly but persistent sheepdog he had managed, with the help of hints about Riesenmoos' strangeness, the dangers of the plateau, and the hopelessness of the Birds' errand, to keep them off the mountain trails. No one else had actually warned them off —not even the Pfnürs—and Perry, however reluctantly, was moved to whisper to Mab, "Orry won't blab all that to him, will she? I think friend Gabriel may be mixed up in all this."

Mab, as Oriole came stalking out the Gappenwirt's front door after them, was direct. "You didn't blab everything, did you?"

"I should think not," Oriole answered stiffly, as she jerked on her fur-lined gloves. "After your Mr. Lanz had the nerve to say that Mama was an idiot to go off and leave us here, I wouldn't give him the satisfaction of telling him *any*thing, let alone your science-fiction foolishnesses."

"What else did he say? Did he ask where she went?"

"No, he didn't ask. He seemed to know." Oriole sniffled audibly and strode ahead, hands thrust deep in her pockets.

"He really does have a nerve. Making a big thing about my not letting you two out of my sight, without a word about why. Except"—she made a mocking face—"except that the ice demons might be out tonight."

Perry noticed Mab's frown and wondered at it. "What did you say to that?" he asked Oriole.

She sniffed. "That you were perfectly capable of dealing with a mere demon. I thanked him to keep his advice to himself." Bringing a rumpled Kleenex up from the depths of her pocket, she blew her nose.

Better and better. If Oriole were angry enough, she could be counted on to dig in her heels against even the best of advice. "Was that all?" Mab ventured.

"Except that he looked as if he'd like to hit me, yes." Oriole kicked violently at the rutted snow and came close to losing her balance on a patch of ice in the middle of the street.

"Here, now! Watch how you go, sweet." Byron, taking heart at Gabriel's fall from favor, tucked Oriole's hand firmly under his elbow and patted it. "We can't have you breaking a leg with no doctor here and the road closed. Besides, you aren't being quite fair to Lanz, are you? It was probably just a heavy-handed Austrian attempt at the light touch. Traditionally the *Eisschemen* do roam above the valley these last nights of Carnival week, you know. Some of the old parish records' accounts are hair-raising. You see . . ." With the competition out of the way, Byron gossiped on in his own heavy-handed attempt at the light touch. For his pains Oriole gave him a withering look, which, happily, he missed.

On Monday morning Oriole was still in a bad temper,

but she seemed to have decided to mend fences with Byron. "It's very sweet of him to offer to take the time to show us the paintings in the church tower when he'd rather be poking around in his dusty manuscripts," she announced firmly. "So we're not going to disappoint him. I have to stop at Metzgers' first for some aspirin, but I'll meet you at the church at ten. *Both* of you."

Perry and Mab dutifully set out ten minutes later, but with no great enthusiasm. By the little wooden shrine at the spot called the Mooserkreuz, halfway down the valley road, they stopped and said with one thought, "Why don't we—"

"You first." Mab grinned.

Perry jammed his hands deep in his jacket pockets. "There's something I'd like to check on those tapes of Byron's. I can always see his old paintings some other time, and he said I could even borrow the recorder now he's not working with it. I think I'll make a dash for it and see if I can find him and get away before Orry turns up. You get away as soon as you can and find Hansl. There's no school today, but he's got to be *some*where. Tell him we'll meet him in the barn after lunch: two o'clock. O.K.? And he has to help us get the gear together for tonight: rucksacks, some food and first-aid stuff—you know."

Mab was worried. "He said he'd go up with us, but he won't if he has to think about it too long. Tonight's a long way off."

Mab was made even more uneasy by the paintings in the bell tower. Now heavily damaged by age and damp, they had once completely circled the walls of the topmost tower room, directly under the bells. Pierced by two windows—

later additions—and covered by flaking layers of whitewash or tempera, the rowdy procession of villagers and mummers had dwindled to the front half of an odd, boat-like chariot, several pairs of dancing feet, a sooty face, a small thicket of smoking torches from under which the torch-bearers were missing—and the Ice Ghosts. There they were, towering over the heads of the rest of the procession and apparently above the reach of the disapproving white-washers. They were exactly as Mab imagined they would be close-to. Blind-eyed, with heavy locks like bristling icicles, hawk-beaked, they groped after the fleeing villagers with horrid daggerish fingers while Byron explained (at great length) the character each figure represented.

"How does it end?" Mab was honestly curious. "And who's the girl on that boat-thing?"

"Ah, there is a real mystery!" Byron was in the sort of unbearably good mood that prevents one from realizing that it is not shared. "I suspect that originally she represented the goddess Perchta, or perhaps Freya, but the old manuscript I'm working on calls her the 'Maiden' or 'Frühling-Mädchen'—the Spring Maiden. As for what happens to her, you'll have to wait until tomorrow." He stole a glance at his watch, asked if there were any more questions, and promptly excused himself to hurry back to his tiny roomful of books in the church crypt.

Oriole lingered a while by the north window, then followed slowly. Mab, curious about what could have held Oriole's attention for so long, hung back, slipping to the window as soon as she was out of sight. Oriole was not normally one for Views.

Below, beyond the last house in the village, a small, quick, blue-sweatered figure strode along the upper road. Gabriel

Lanz, with his skis on his shoulder. Mab gave a motherly sigh. Poor Orry! It *was* too bad about Gabriel. He was definitely fishy, even if he did have a nice face. Mab watched him pass the Vogelerfeld lift and frowned. Past the Vogelerfeld, there was nowhere to go but the Hochgebirgsschule Pfnür. Everything always seemed to come back to the Pfnürschule.

So, of course, did the Pfnürs. While Mab watched, their bright blue Ghia purred into sight below the church and swung onto the Moosweg, climbing steadily out of the village. From the top of the bell tower it was difficult to tell if Gabriel was hidden from the approaching car by the rise and dip of the road until suddenly, unexpectedly, he plunged off the road, rolling—skis and all—down a steep bank. At the bottom he lay very still under a clump of scraggly bushes. It had all happened so fast that if Mab had blinked, she might have missed it; and having seen, she didn't know what to make of it. What could Gabriel Lanz be up to that the Pfnürs oughtn't to see?

"Mab? You up there?" Oriole's voice floated up through the well where the bell ropes hung. "Come along down. Herr Glöckner wants to lock the tower."

Mab moved reluctantly, wanting to see whether the Ghia slowed down as it came abreast of that spot on the road. She could not be sure. "Coming," she called mendaciously, and stayed to watch the car out of sight.

Puzzled, but dimly cheered, she descended the rickety staircase with dragging footsteps. It looked as if a little recasting might be in order. Was Gabriel the Reluctant Villain and Oriole a Doubting Heroine? A more cooperative heroine might have managed "Tormented" or "Tragic," but cautious doubt—perhaps a touch of wistfulness—was about the best that could be expected of Oriole. Gabriel—by the time Mab reached the foot of the stairs, Gabriel had been re-revised to The Enigmatic Stranger.

What *was* he doing in Riesenmoos?

Perry looked around him. "Hey, this is great." He unfastened the cover of the heavy portable tape recorder and set it carefully to one side on the hard earth. "When this idea up and hit me on the head, I didn't know if there *was* any bare ground around. There are lots of rocks sticking up out of the snow outside, but rock isn't as good a sound conductor. Even with the ground frozen hard, this ought to work."

Mab and Hansl squatted beside him in the gloom of the storeroom under the Strumpfs' dairy. Grissel shifted and stamped overhead, and around them crowded stack upon stack of neatly cut firewood and farm implements—plough, harrows, rakes and mattocks—carefully oiled against the winter damp. Mab held the flashlight so that Perry could read the labels on the recorder's dials.

"Did you tell Byron you knew how to work this thing?" Mab was doubtful. "And how come old Bussfudget let you trot off with his precious recorder without an explanation?"

"I have a reliable face. Besides, I do know how to work it. Tigger Schultz's dad has one just like it." Perry squinted as he threaded a new reel of tape between the magnets. "Byron's not so bad. I mean, he can bore you cross-eyed, but he didn't even ask me what I wanted it for. He just said, 'Get it back by four o'clock.'" Perry slipped the end of the tape into the take-up reel and, with a push of a button, wound a short length around it. "You know, I was right about his Riesenmoos tapes—the ones he complained were spotty with static. Old Byron labels everything: subject, speaker, place recorded, time recorded. I checked back, and sure enough, he was recording the staticked bits Friday morning at just about the time that toothache hit me first. The same pattern, too. Now, no nice, normal radio station can do that. It's got to be something close by and really powerful." Unwinding the cord from around the microphone, he laid it, mouthpiece down, on the hard earth. Then he took off his jacket, folded it, and placed it like a blanket over the mike.

Hansl watched all this suspiciously. "I understand nothing of this. You are saying that it is not the Ice Ghosts but some electrical thing which haunts us. Perhaps it is so, but then why could not the demons themselves be—electrical? I have seen them. Sometimes they shine even when the moon is dark, and they are real enough. Mab has seen that they are real. Has she told you that she has seen the Ghost above the Riesenalm?"

"Yes, well, she did." Perry was cautious. "But they might be men, you know. Dressed up like your Carnival ghosts, maybe even wierder. Can you think of a better way of keeping people tucked up snug at home? Who's going to go snooping up the mountain if he thinks the goblins are going to get him?"

Hansl was unconvinced. "But why do you wish to listen to the ground with that machine? Electricity will not travel through the earth."

"Nope, it doesn't. Look, you two, I'm going to switch this on now. Don't move, don't even breathe if you can help it. I've set the pitch and everything so the mike is as sensitive as I can get it. O.K.? O.K. *Go.*"

For thirty seconds the cold storeroom was silent except

for Grissel's movements overhead and, once, the tripping patter of the goat's feet. Then, switching off the mike, Perry rewound the tape to its starting point and pushed the PLAY button. The volume he turned on full.

At first there was only the grainy, magnified crackle of the background "silence," and then abruptly, like a heavy blow upon their eardrums, came a thunderous, steady *Thrummthrumm-thrumm-thrummthrumm*. It set the children's teeth to chattering and heads to throbbing. Above, the animals could be heard bumping rhythmically against their stalls.

"Turn it down," Mab screeched. "Down!" She reached toward the controls. Her temples ached fiercely. Even her elbows and knees seemed to throb.

Perry held her off. "I've got it . . . there. Man, has this rig got amplification! I guess I'd better erase the tape, or it'll give old Byron a heart attack."

Hansl drew a deep breath. "*Ach*, it is good my papa and mama are not in the house. Mama would think the demons were hammering on the roof."

"What *was* that?" Mab demanded. A body could die of frustration before Perry got around to explanations.

"Generators," said her brother, wisely. "Five dollars says it's some kind of powerful electrical generator. Maybe two or three. If the whole mountain is riddled with caves, they'd act like echo chambers, but even allowing for that, it's sure some vibration. Whatever goes on up there must take a heck of a lot of power." He shrugged back into his windbreaker and zipped it up against the cold.

"That was only vibration? How much magnified?" Hansl asked shrewdly. When Perry admitted that he had no way of telling, the smaller boy unexpectedly stripped off his mittens, stretched himself flat on the earthen floor, and put his ear and fingertips to the ground. After a few moments he scrambled up, his eyes gleaming as much with excitement as from the glow of Mab's flashlight. "It is true. The *thrumm-thrumm*, it is there, like an ache in the ground."

Mab, not to be outdone, listened herself. "You know," she said afterward, "I bet that's what sets everybody on edge so, even the animals. You had it up loud enough to turn a body's brains to mush, but even when you don't know you're hearing it, it must be nibbling at your nerves."

"At some times it is worse than at others. Perhaps it is that it does not always work at full power," Hansl said.

Perry nodded. "It would be a lot worse than it is now if they were transmitting. They'd have to pull out all the stops to get that kind of juice."

Hansl spoke dreamily, talking half to himself. "The great, stumpy footprints I have seen of the Ice Ghosts . . . They are round, dragging prints that do not sink into the snowdrifts. They could be some sort of snowshoe, *vielleicht?* Only smaller and more round."

Mab gave a small crow of delight. "Right on! That's got to be it. And we know exactly where they're from!"

Perry gave her a blank look.

"The Pfnürschule. On the center wall in that equipment room."

He nodded thoughtfully. "They *were* oval-shaped, weren't they? And smaller than ordinary snowshoes. Sort of like oversize tennis rackets without handles."

Hansl had halted at the storeroom door. "The Pfnürs? You are saying it is the Pfnürs who do this evil on the mountain. How can that be, when they are so good to Riesenmoos?" He hesitated. "Perhaps . . . perhaps if there is this great electrical machine, it is made for some good reason. It could be so, no? I cannot think why the Pfnürs would do a thing which was not good. Why should they do so?"

"For money," Mab almost said, but she caught herself. "Who knows? Maybe it's not them," she said evasively. "Or even Gabriel. It might be some of the Pfnürschule instructors. They were a pretty unfriendly looking bunch." She knew, without Perry's skeptical look, how unlikely it was that anyone but the Pfnürs themselves could have moved heavy equipment into the Eiswinkel without detection—even piecemeal or over a long time—but Hansl's loyalties were not likely to be shaken by guesses.

"Gabriel?" Hansl pulled the door open with an angry tug and stepped out into the snow. "Next you will say that my papa knows of these things, or Herr Metzger, or even old Herr Glöckner. It is foolishness. Gabriel is my friend."

Mab followed him out into the long shadows of afternoon. "It was only an idea. He was heading up the Pfnürschule road about two hours ago, and he made sure the Pfnürs didn't see him when they drove past. He might've been going up the mountain. He was carrying his skis and a rucksack."

"Very well." Hansl was stiffly polite. "I owe you because we have feared to say your papa stayed with us. And I have gived my word. Tonight I will take you to the Eisschemenhöhle and tomorrow, if you wish, to the plateau. You will see that you are mistaken. If we are eaten by the ice demons, at least you will see."

Hansl was as good as his word. By nine o'clock Oriole and Byron were engrossed in the Gappenwirt's soufflé dessert, two bolster-pillow shapes slumbered convincingly in Mab's and Perry's beds, and the three climbers had come up the steep gully below the Eisschemenhöhle to the great gates of the cave itself.

The cavern's entrance was a broad arch some twelve feet high, and the gates spanning it were set well in under the eaves of the hill. The children sat for a moment in the shadow before the gates to catch their breath and looked down the deep cleft into the moon-washed valley, where the tall trees grew like patches of black velvet on fields of moon-gray silk. Nothing could have looked more peaceful.

"They're starting it up again," Perry muttered. Scooping together a handful of snow to hold against his jaw, he rose to take a closer look at the iron gates, which loomed gray against the darkness now that their eyes had become a bit accustomed to the gloom. They had been finely wrought, with heavy supports and intricate strapwork—knots and twinings of such elaborate design that a cat would have had a tight squeeze of it to get through. They were fastened by a heavy chain wrapped around the two center posts and secured by a large old-fashioned padlock that must have measured five inches across its face. Mab, running her gloved hands over the strapwork, felt the faint tingle of vibration.

Hansl was nervous. "You have seen what you wished to see. There is nothing here. Please, now we must go."

Mab squinted. "Maybe we could climb up over the top. There's a space between the top bar and the roof of the passage—right in the middle there."

Perry shook his head. "Maybe you could make it, but I sure couldn't. I'd get stuck. You and Hansl can have a try, though."

Hansl regarded Mab with alarm. "You do not mean to try? What if you needed to come out again in a great

118

hurry? It would be an impossibility."

"Well, there's no point in just standing out here, and it seems an awful waste just to go back to bed," argued Mab practically. "Besides, caution butters no parsley, as they say." She jangled the chain, then bent to peer at the padlock.

"Par*snips*." Perry laughed, and then winced as his tooth gave another twinge. "If Hansl won't go, you can't go in by yourself. If you fell or got hurt, who'd know where to find you?"

Mab wasn't listening. She slipped off a glove and touched a dark smear on the face of the padlock. "Look, it's been oiled." Her voice dropped to a whisper. "Shine a light over here."

The boys bent close, shielding Perry's flashlight beam with their bodies from any chance viewer on the slopes below. Mab pointed out bright marks around the keyhole. The padlock had been opened often and recently. Hansl, who had come the last half mile with his fingers crossed inside his mittens and muttering under his breath an old charm against demons, cheered up considerably. Demons had no need of keys.

Nor did Mab, as it turned out. She fingered a flange just below the keyhole and the shackle, astonishingly, clicked open. Like many very old padlocks, this one did not lock automatically upon being snapped shut, but required a turn of the key. "Won't you come into my parlor," Mab chortled, as she set about unwinding the chain.

"You cut that out." Perry switched off the flashlight. "Hurry it up, and let's get inside before somebody sees us." In the light's brief glow, he had noticed footprints in the drifted snow. Large ones. Slipping inside after Mab and Hansl, he drew the gates together and hastily arranged the chain and lock as they had been before. "A quick look around. That's all, O.K.?"

The air inside the cave mouth was icy, and the sloping floor even icier. Mab, caught off balance, slipped downward in the darkness and crashed with a muffled exclamation, into a great heap of objects that bounced and creaked and went rolling out from under her. "Don't turn on the light from up there," she hissed. "I'm O.K. I think I fell in a pile of baskets."

Hansl felt his way along the wall. "It must be the baskets which we have brought yesterday with the offerings. But we left them on the outside."

"Well, they're inside now—and empty. We'd better stack them back up, but be careful. It's slithery over here."

Perry advanced cautiously. "I can see a little now."

"I do not like this," Hansl muttered. "How if someone comes? How are we to get out then?"

"If you're so worried, maybe you'd better keep a lookout from outside," Perry grumbled from somewhere deeper in the passage.

"I am not afraid," Hansl said stiffly. "I wish only to be practical."

"Oh, sure." Perry was uneasy himself. The passage floor was icy, but except for the first few yards, it had been strewn with sand and was not dangerous. *Except.* Except that a sanded floor suggested a regular traffic through the Eisschemenhöhle gate. The children could not use their lights for fear of being seen, and without lights, they could go no further. "Just when it starts getting interesting," he complained.

"*Piggy.*"

Mab's whisper had the urgency of a shriek, and at the

same moment a faint thumping, churning sound caught his ear. Perry turned and was just able, in the faint reflected moonlight, to make out Mab and Hansl, crouched down behind what must have been several years' accumulation of baskets. Mab pointed frantically toward the grillwork of the massive gates. One brief look, and Perry too had scrambled into the scant shelter behind the jumbled heap of basketry.

In the bright moonlight outside the gate, snow spilled down from somewhere above on the gully's slope, rose in a cloud, shimmered, and settled. Where the cloud had risen, stood two tall white figures, indistinct at first against the bright slope, then looming darker against the brightness as they shuffled toward the gate. Mab and Hansl shrank down against the icy wall and concentrated on looking as basket-like as possible, but Perry kept to his feet, shrinking back into a small recess behind a billow in the ice wall. He could not take his eyes off the towering icicle-crowned apparitions standing so still outside the gate, but he did put up his hands to shade them, as if, like a cat's, they might shine in the dark and betray him. The silence lengthened. His stomach tightened sickeningly.

The taller of the two Ice Ghosts reached out a gauntleted hand to the chain on the gate. "*Es ist nicht geschlossen,*" it intoned in a deep and horridly hollow voice. The chain undone, the gates swung silently inward. Perry, whose knees at least were still in working order, slid silently down the wall and groped for the Mabbit's hand. Neither was afterward very clear as to who was reassuring whom.

"Hah!" The second ghost delivered himself of a gusty sigh and proceeded to remove his grisly head and shoulders and prop them against the wall opposite. He then dug into a deep pocket, brought out a small flask, and took a long swallow. *"So, gut!"* He wiped his mouth appreciatively. "Now all I need is a tall beer and a steaming bowl of that good *gulyas* soup!"

nine

"If the dragon smells that brandy on you, you're in the *gulyas* soup yourself," the first ghost observed sourly. His voice came from the region where the giant's breastbone might have been supposed to be.

"No fear. I always keep my distance. Here, give a hand. I'll have to put this cursed thing back on. It's too awkward to carry."

"Put it on yourself, you lazy dog. It's not heavy." The first ghost turned his key in the lock and stumped off into the darkness. The second followed, untangling the ghostly streamers that flapped from the mask's high, hunched shoulders and grumbling to himself.

The children stared at each other numbly. They were locked in, and the key was rapidly disappearing into the mountain.

Mab moved first, gingerly, careful not to let her boots scrape against the ice. Her whisper floated back into the gloom. "It's locked, all right. What do we do now?"

Perry was hesitant. With their bridge burnt behind them, he felt a considerable falling away of enthusiasm. Mab might be able to climb the gate and squeeze out over the top, to go for help, but who would believe her? Oriole and Byron, but a fat lot of help they would be.

It was Hansl who decided. After five fearful winters spent in dread of the Watcher on the Riesenalm, a two-piece ice ghost with a thirst for beer was nothing but an immense relief. He scrambled to his feet, dancing up and down a little to drive away the prickles of cold. As he jiggled, his words came in frosty puffs. "We follow. What else can we do? No one will come to help us. We will not be missed. Your sister will think you asleep, and Mama thinks I spend the night at Fritz Baumann's. But we must hurry. Do you see, far along there? They are having light somehow."

They were indeed having light somehow. The passage sloped downward in darkness for fifty or sixty yards to a point where a string of dim lights glowed on the cavern wall. The cavern itself opened up somewhere ahead, for there was no reflection from the lights on ice or rock, only a dim, yellowish glow. As the children watched, they winked out. Further along, others winked on. "Come," Hansl urged. Taking Mab's hand, he led the way into the mountain at a cautious half-trot, guiding himself by trailing his other hand along the wall. Perry, his mind a muddle of misgivings and highly disturbing excitement, trotted obediently behind.

The children had not gone far when they sensed that the ice walls had given way to rock and that they were no longer in a passageway, but in some larger hall. The ground underfoot was no longer sand patched with treacherous slickness, but rock, and the chill breeze died to a whisper.

The distant lights flicked out.

"They're too far ahead. We'll never catch up if we can't see where to put our stupid feet," Mab complained. As if to prove her point, she stumbled awkwardly and came close to turning her ankle in a small pothole. "How do the lights keep moving along with them?" she gasped.

"I don't know . . ." Perry's vagueness had a thoughtful ring. Slipping off one glove, he searched through his pockets and brought out a grubby blue handkerchief. A double thickness, fastened over the lens of his flashlight with a rubber band from a pocket collection of useful oddments, dimmed its light to a pale blue glow. "There has to be a switch here somewhere." He played the light along the near wall and came to an abrupt, staring stop.

A tall woman stood no more than fifteen feet away, in the shadows at the edge of the blue light. The children could just make out the long, pale hair that rippled to her ankles, but her face was hidden by her upraised arms. Beyond, other dim figures peopled the shadows along the wall.

"It—it is the Ice Brides." Hansl's courage began to shrivel a little around the edges.

But only for a moment. "She's not ice, she's stone." Mab giggled in relief. "Only stone. And look: she has a light switch where her belly button ought to be!"

So she had. An electrician with a rude sense of humor had strung his wires around the uncannily human limestone column like a slender belt, with the switch in the place of a low-slung buckle. "For Pete's sake!" was the only comment Perry could manage. Mab stepped forward to press the switch, apologizing solemnly, "Excuse me, Ma'am"—and nimbly dodged the kick her brother aimed at her ankle.

The lights—a string of naked bulbs no brighter than twenty-five watts—winked the cavern into shadowy life. Its uneven floor was perhaps fifty feet across and stretched lengthwise fifty yards or more to the darkness at the end of the string of lights. The ceiling above where the children stood was no more than fifteen feet high, but toward the center of the room, it rose beyond the light's reach. Down that sloping surface, long centuries of seeping water had dripped the limestone into the columns that grew along the wall like tall, slender figures. In the light, dim as it was, the wire-belted lady lost much of the woman-shape she had suggested in the muffled glow of the flashlight, and her companions blurred into no more than stone pillars rippling down the cavern wall. It was no wonder that earlier visitors to the Eisschemenhöhle, armed only with candles or crude lanterns, had turned heel at the sight. Braver souls, venturing out into the wide room itself, picking a way through the stony rubble that littered much of the floor, would not have gone far before they too turned and ran; for three massive columns waited near the cavern's center, thick-bodied, heavy-limbed, with rootlike feet and stony locks that clustered like icicles around shadowy, gap-mouthed faces. The stalactites and stalagmites that had grown together to make the great pillars had in one of them grown in such a way that the stone giant actually seemed to clutch a wavy-bladed sword in one huge misshapen hand.

"So! These are the Ice Giants." Hansl picked his way around the feet of the largest. "Not only are they not demons, they are not even ice. It is foolish, perhaps, but I

126

could wish they had been ice. It is this way disappointing, much like finding out that it is Herr Glöckner who plays at being St. Nicholas on Twelfth Night. But you will think that is very silly of me."

"N-not really." Mab's teeth chattered. "But could we think about it while we're going? It g-gets *cold* standing still. Besides, it must be getting late . . ."

The lights went out.

"Who—who did that?" Hansl's whisper was loud in the stillness. "Where are you?"

"Not so loud. We're over here." Perry switched his flashlight on and moved out until the muffled light touched the stones and sand at Hansl's feet. "Can you see? Well, come on, then."

"Who *did* switch the light off?" Mab asked, trembling, when the boys regained the wall. "Somebody up ahead's watching us, aren't they?"

"I don't think so." Perry answered as firmly as he could manage. "If they knew we were here, I expect they'd just come and collect us." He stood undecided for a moment, then brightened. "Wait a sec. That switch is a push one, not the flip kind, isn't it? Maybe it—" He felt along the wire for the switch. "Yeah, it's the delay kind. You push in, and a minute later it pops out again. They have them in the upstairs hallway at the Gappenwirt—to save electricity. Byron says they're timed so you get halfway to the bathroom or to the top of the stairs, and they go off. I'd guess these are rigged to stay on long enough for any-one passing through to reach the next section before this one snaps off."

"Then it does not matter that we have lost the false ghosts. Push it again," Hansl urged. "We will follow the lights into the mountain."

"And without getting lost down the wrong passage." Mab jiggled up and down to keep warm. "Gabriel said these caves must be like honeycombs, remember? Go on, push it."

Perry shook his head. "We'd better not. If we could see these lights from clear back by the gate, they can see them from up ahead, too. We'll be safer with the flashlight. We can't get lost. The wires are still here to follow."

"But we won't be able to see the caves," protested Mab.

"Next time you can ask for the architecture tour," Perry said grimly. He pulled her after him.

Without the electrical wiring for a guide, the children would have been hopelessly lost. From the changing echo of their footsteps, they knew when they passed from a large chamber into a smaller, but only in the narrower passageways did the dim blue light show both walls and the rock above. The hemmed-in feeling in the passages was a welcome one after trailing a pale glowworm of a light through a blackness full of distant echoes. Here and there the wires and bulbs were strung across open space, sagging from one pillar to the next, and then plunging down a rippled stair into another narrow, high-roofed passage. Normally, Mab's sense of space and direction was uncanny—she played the Blind Game so well that it was always a little eerie watching her. Instinct told her now that their path was slowly bending to the north. After climbing steadily for perhaps a quarter of a mile, it began by gradual stages to slope downward; but the route was so crooked that she soon lost count of the turns and ups and downs and began to mistrust her instinct.

"Mustn't think about the outside shape like on a map," she muttered padding along at Perry's heels. "It gets all muddled if you try to think about both at the same time. Just keep the inside straight." The inside shape. The inside shape was as complicated as the inside of Oöstructure II, —if not more so. There had to be other exits. The Eisriesenhöhle gate was too exposed to view to be the main entrance.

"Hold it." Perry snapped off the flashlight. "There's a light up ahead. We'll have to feel our way along the wall. O.K.? Now *really* make like mice."

"Make like mice?" Hansl's whisper was bewildered. "What is that?"

The closer they came to it, the more the light appeared to be coming up out of the floor at the end of the chamber. The children moved cautiously along the wall, carefully feeling ahead with each foot before taking a step. Their path bent and tilted narrowly downward a scant fifteen yards from the light that glowed beyond the knife-edge blackness marking the end of the chamber floor. A few yards further down the narrow ramp, around an abrupt corner, and they would have found themselves on a brightly-lit lower level with their two friends from the gate. Perry, hearing the voices that rumbled below, shot out an arm to stop Mab and Hansl. Back on the upper level, they crawled across to the floor's edge.

"Keep down," Perry breathed. "Keep your faces out of the light."

The room below was a gigantic pothole, carved deep into the limestone by some long-ago river. Twenty-five feet below, three wooden chairs and a table with a hot plate sat near one wall. Four grisly Ice Ghost masks leaned on their icicle-streamered frameworks along the wall nearby. Directly across from the spot where the children crouched, they saw a gaping black hole in the face of the end wall of the main chamber. An ancient river once had poured from it. Now, a ladder led down to the sandy floor of the pothole. It was clearly the opening into another passage, and anyone coming along it would have looked directly across at the children. Hansl drew back, and Mab pulled off her red hood and flattened down, hoping that in their dark ski clothes they might pass for an outcropping of rock, but Perry inched forward until his nose touched the edge. Had either of the men below glanced up, they could not have missed the gleam of his blond hair, but Perry meant to see as much as possible before turning back to the gate and sending Mab and Hansl over the top for help.

Two additional passageways opened off the sunken room. The one at the right angled downward. Another, to the left of the ladder, sloped upward. From each ran the wires stapled to the rock wall that meant a chain of lights. The cable running below the wires was explained by the telephone on the wall between the two passages, beside the ladder. One of the two men listened, nodding, at the phone. The other poured himself a cup of reheated coffee from a battered enamel pan on the hot plate. Both were dressed in trim white snow gear.

"*Ja, ja.* We have seen only Karl and Rudi and our other friend. They came from below just as we came in. *Ja,* about four or five minutes ago. They went on up. *Ach, so!* Yes, we heard. Which way did he come in?"

The second man raised his eyebrows questioningly at

this, and his companion listened a moment and then pointed to the ladder and the passage above. "Who, Herman?" he asked with a grin at his partner. "*Nein*, he has gone down already to the kitchen. I go too as soon as I hang up. What?" He frowned. "But that is impossible. We locked the gate and came directly here. We would have seen if . . . *Ja.* Of course. I will check and report back." Hanging up, he reached down a heavy battery lantern from a bracket above the telephone and checked its beam. To Herman, he growled, "You'd better be off to your supper. If I had known there was still work to do, I would not have said you were gone."

"What's happened?" Herman tossed the dregs of the coffee against the wall and wiped his mouth on the back of his hand.

"*Ach*, they have intruders on the brain. Weibel says that after we came through from the gate, the monitor board up in the control room showed that a set of lights in the first chamber switched on again. But it cannot have been an intruder. We were careless about the gate going out, perhaps, but if anyone had come in, we would have passed them, *nicht wahr?* Depend upon it, it is some trick of defective wiring. A waste of time, but I must go out to check. Go along with you! I have said that you are on your way down, and the dragon will be expecting you."

Finishing off his own coffee, he headed for the ramp to the upper level and the path back to the gate.

The children froze, terrified. They were trapped on an open expanse of floor with not a pillar, boulder, or pebble to hide behind. Mab was afraid to move an eyelash for fear the guard would hear it. Dim light or no, they must be clearly visible. Fortunately, he did not look back. Walking briskly, he played the powerful beam of his lantern over the rock formations at the other end of the room, then disappeared into the passage beyond.

"*Quick!*"

The children darted toward the ramp, reaching it just as the lights snapped off. On the threshold of the guards' room, they hesitated.

"Which way?" Hansl was pale but excited.

"Up." Mab slipped past Perry and across the room. "Down is to the kitchen, or whatever, but *auf* is to the *Kontrol Raum*. I understood that much." She peered up the *auf* passage.

Perry followed. "Well, we sure as heck can't get out. We might as well go whole hog and find out what's going on."

"Speaking of which—" Mab paused in the darkness of the climbing passage. "Everything seems quieter." She laid her hand against the rock wall. "Something's still vibrating, but I don't *hear* it any more. Is your toothache still on?"

"Not now. It stopped five or ten minutes ago. Man, do you know what we almost did? We almost came all the way in using their old lights. They wouldn't have blamed *that* on defective wiring. Dumb luck, that's us. It's a pretty sneaky system they've got. While you're saving electricity, you're keeping tabs on where people are."

Hansl looked back toward the glow from the guard room with a worried frown. It was all much too easy. In a doubtful whisper, he ventured, "There cannot *really* be a dragon down the other way. Can there?"

The going in the steep, tunnel-like passage was much faster and easier, even though Perry had added to the cov-

132

ering on his flashlight a dark wool sock rooted out from under the first-aid kit in Mab's knapsack. To his impatient demand to know why she was carrying not only extra socks, a packet of raisins, seven chocolate bars, and a can of lemonade, but also a pocket sewing kit, a felt laundry marker, extra shoelaces (three pairs), and a fat coil of nylon rope, she only shrugged. "I thought we might need them. Besides, the rope was Mama's idea. At least, I found it in her big suitcase, so she must have thought it would be useful around mountains and caves. Well, it *might*." Perry buckled the knapsack shut with a sigh.

The narrow, low-ceilinged corridor climbed gradually but steadily and in a relatively straight line for perhaps a quarter of a mile. By degrees the incline leveled out. The passage widened and from time to time turned a shallow corner. The walls, at irregular intervals, had been worn away by heavy water seepage from above, carving out small holes and niches and even shallow alcoves. A number of these held shovels and buckets of sand, an oddity explained when Perry's dim light picked out large oil drums stacked three high in rows that stretched back into the darkness in two deeper alcoves. Fire extinguishers hung in brackets in several smaller niches.

Ahead, a faint light gleamed, and a man's laughter rang out.

Perry stopped short. "Er—maybe we ought to scout out a place where we could hole up for a little while?" He tried to sound cautious rather than nervous. "We must be getting pretty close to whatever it is. They only stopped transmitting a little while ago, so there must still be a lot of them up ahead. We'd have a better chance for a look around if we waited until some of them clear out. What do you say? It's warmer in here, so it shouldn't be too bad."

Mab and Hansl whispered their agreement and moved ahead slowly, following Perry's lead. With the light so cautiously muffled up, they could see barely five feet ahead. Its dim, bluish glow slid across the walls, probed weakly down a narrow passage falling away to the right, and came to rest on a hole no more than four feet high in which several small wooden crates were stacked. Perry motioned with the light, and Mab stooped to edge in past the crates. In a moment she was peering out again like a small bright-eyed animal from its nest. "There's plenty of room. We could—"

The rest went unsaid. Far ahead, a piercing klaxon blared twice, and then twice again. The scuffling noises and the clang of metal on rock that followed the alarm sounded uncomfortably close. Mab moved back quickly, and Hansl ducked to follow her in. "*Perry!*"

"It's O.K.," came the whispered answer. "The lights up ahead've gone off. Whoever it was is going the other way. If we go on a way, we're sure to find another hole. Maybe we can get close enough to hear something." His old, cautious self struggled for the upper hand, but curiosity was stronger.

Beyond the next turning, the passage widened into a long, irregular room. Along both sides smaller rooms and dim galleries opened black mouths. One alcove held two odd chairs, a table, and a telephone, another a battered camp bed. There was nothing remotely like a hiding place, and at the sound of a bell and more shouts far ahead, Perry snapped off the flashlight.

"Mabbit? Hang onto my coat. I can feel the way along

here. Better not use the light." He groped a few cautious yards.

"Look, if they come back this way before we find a place to sit tight, everybody back to the other hole. O.K. Hansl, Mab? *Mab? What's wrong?*" At Mab's sudden intake of breath he reached out to where she should have been. "*Where are you?*" The hand that held the flashlight came up against the wall with a nasty crack, and the flashlight dropped to the floor with a dull clatter and rolled. "Oh, *damn!*"

"Peregrine Bird, you *swore!*" Mab's indignant hiss came from ahead and to his right.

"Well, why didn't you answer?" he grated back. Sucking a scraped knuckle, he stooped to feel for the flashlight. "You were supposed to keep behind. The way you sounded, I thought something grabbed you."

"It kind of did," she whispered nervously. "I mean, I think I stepped on something."

"What's that supposed to mean? And how the heck are we supposed to see what it is in the dark?" He could not find the flashlight.

Mab's hand met the shoulder of his jacket and held tight. "Perry?" she said in a stifled whisper. "I think I stepped on some*body*."

Perry straightened abruptly. "Don't be disgusting," he said firmly. "It was probably a patch of soft sand. Why'd you have to go poking ahead? Here, hold still while I get the other flashlight out of your knapsack."

"It didn't feel like a patch of sand. It felt like a leg with a boot on it," Mab snapped.

Hansl moved past without waiting for the light, and a

moment later, a little breathless, called softly, "She is right. Someone lies here. Perhaps he has fallen and hurt himself."

Perry rooted out Mab's second sock and pulled it over the flashlight. In a moment he was beside Hansl and the figure stretched face-down on the floor. The pale wash of light showed a man, blond, his face smeared with dirt or soot. He was dressed in dark blue and wearing ski boots. A red instructor's stripe glowed on one sleeve of the dark sweater.

"Gabriel!" Hansl drew back, bewildered. "What is he doing here? He . . . he is not dead, is he?"

Mab, suddenly practical, slipped one small hand under Gabriel's head to feel for the pulse in his neck. It was strong and steady, if her whispered answer was not. "He's all right."

"What's the matter with him, then?" Perry knelt, keeping a nervous eye and ear cocked in the direction in which the voices had disappeared. With his help, Gabriel—who was even heavier than he looked—was rolled onto his side, his back against the rock wall. The children saw, almost with relief, that his hands were tied. That could only mean that he was no friend to the Ice Ghosts and whatever they were up to deep in the mountain. It occurred to Perry that Gabriel must have been the cause of the remark about "intruders on the brain" they had overheard earlier. If he knew a way out that did not lead back to the gate . . .

That hope was short-lived. No amount of shaking stirred him. Whoever had put him to sleep had not much cared whether he woke up again. An ugly red welt ran from his temple down along his chin, and he bled from a nasty gash in the scalp above his temple.

"Maybe it's not as bad as it looks," Mab faltered. "I bled

like anything that time I fell and hit my head on the sidewalk roller skating. It didn't even hurt much. Not really," she added hopefully. Slipping her arms free of the knapsack, she rooted in it for the first-aid kit.

"No, no bandage," Hansl warned. "We must leave him here. We cannot move him, and a bandage would shout that we are here." He took the gauze bandage from Mab, replacing it in the tin box. "Especially an American bandage. Ours are not like these."

Perry wavered as he saw Mab's mulish look; but any argument was stopped by the dim glow that sprang up beyond the turning in the passage ahead. A shout echoed, distorted by distance and the tunnel's turnings. Perry had located his own flashlight with the help of Mab's, and now, thrusting hers at her with a breathless, "The box hole! Quick!", he pelted back the way they had come, Hansl close at his heels. Mab snatched up her knapsack to follow, and as abruptly put it down again. The voices ahead were louder, but there was still a minute or two of safety. Kneeling, she quickly untwisted the ends of the wire binding Gabriel's wrists, unwound several turns, and did them up again loosely.

"In case you wake up," she whispered, scrambling to her feet. It took several sharp tugs to roll him face down, as they had found him. As she pulled frantically, it sounded as if he moaned a little, but there was no time to be sure.

There was no time to do anything. The lights came on.

Mab looked around in panic. If she ran, the searchers were sure to be in sight before she cleared the light at the end of the chamber. Snatching up the knapsack and her flashlight, she ran for the closest of the shadowy openings in the rock wall. It looked large and dark enough to be the

137

opening into another passage, but she was brought up short within ten feet by a wooden barrier. A door, in fact. Her fingers scrabbled at the rough wood, but there was no handle, only a keyhole. A keyhole and a squarish window cut high in the door's center. "Oh, what'll I *do?*" she moaned, half aloud.

Reaching up, she ran her hand around the edges of the hole. She was small enough, and it felt large enough, but she was unable to pull herself up to climb through. Not without a hand up, or something to stand on. More frustrated than frightened, she shrank into the more shadowy corner. "Rats! Leave it to old fish-face, soup-face, pie-face Mavis," she whispered, not very sensibly. *"Rats!"*

"Mabbit?"

A shadow only a little less dark than the darkness moved at the hatch in the door. Mab froze. The searchers were close enough for voices to carry distinctly. One, sharper and higher than the others, crackled out with, "Hurry, you fools! How long does it take you to search a few rabbit holes."

But Mab did not hear. She scarcely breathed. It was an age before she could make her thumb press the button on the flashlight, and another before she managed to raise the beam to where a familiar pair of astonished blue eyes peered out over an unfamiliar gingery beard.

"Daddy!"

ten

Professor Bird wasted no time. "Pass that rucksack through," he ordered brusquely. "Your jacket, too. It's too bulky. Quickly, sweetheart. You may be a 'pigment of my imagination,' as you used to put it, but we'll clear that up later. Right. Now, give me both hands and *don't try to help.*" He grasped her wrists and she his, aerialist-fashion. "That's right," he breathed, pulling steadily upward despite the awkward angle. "Keep limp. Better a few bruises than banging your boots against the door, trying to help." Once Mab's head and shoulders were inside, he slipped his hands under her arms and lifted her through easily.

"Oh, Daddy! You *are* all right. We *knew* you were." Mab wrapped her arms around her father, but he as quickly unwrapped them. "No time for that now, peanut. You have to get out of sight. Here you go: under the cot." He steered her to the right, and when her shins came up against the low cot, pushed her down and thrust the rucksack and jacket under after her. "Not a word. Don't even breathe."

Mab obeyed, shrinking as close to the wall as possible, at the sound of heavy footsteps. Her father, moving quickly in the dark, pulled a blanket free of the foot of the cot and draped it so that it dragged on the floor, hiding Mab's feet from any prying flashlight. Then he eased himself onto the sagging cot and lay quietly with his arms behind his head. Mab, half squashed, made herself as flat as she could and pulled the jacket under her cheek for a pillow.

Seconds later, a bright beam speared through the aperture, swept the rough walls of the narrow chamber, and fixed on Professor Bird's face. The Professor started, blinked, and put up his hands to shield his eyes from the glare. "What—what is it?" he mumbled in sleepy irritation. "What do you want?"

Mab's breath caught at the familiar smoothness of the answering voice. "Do not discompose yourself, Herr Professor," it said. "It is a matter of no urgency. Still, perhaps . . . You have not by chance heard something these past five minutes. Someone passing? A light, perchance?" Doktor Pfnür was as gently formal as if he were paying a polite social call.

"No," Professor Bird drawled. "Not that I'd tell you if I had. What's the trouble, Herr Doktor? Another unwelcome guest?"

"Perhaps. Perhaps not. I have been informed that one of the guards found something in the passage that leads to the Eisschemenhöhle Gate. A trifle, you understand. A lady's handkerchief."

Mab's throat tightened. *Handkerchief.* Where was hers? Oriole's, rather. She had run out of Kleenex and borrowed one of Oriole's hankies. Her fingers inched toward the jacket, but its pockets were folded under, out of reach.

If it *was* Orry's handkerchief, her initials were on it. *A.B.* With luck, Doktor Pfnür might not guess that Oriole was A. B. and not O. B.

Herr Doktor Pfnür considered. "It is possible, of course, that one of the guards now off duty could have dropped it. Even our friend Lanz. A souvenir of some sweet *Mädchen* in Werfenweng, perhaps. A charming explanation, *nicht wahr?* You see, I tell you everything, Herr Professor, but never once do you return the favor."

Professor Bird's voice was even. "That's right. What have you done with young Lanz?"

"Questions, always questions." Pfnür's voice sharpened as he moved away from the door to direct the searchers. "What are you standing about for? Karl, Rudi—check the storage rooms and the top of the shaft. And take care in there, you fools. Sepp, you will go to the guard room with Heinz and see that it is not left unattended again. Willi and Franz: I depend upon you to search every smallest crack between here and the guard room. The Frau Doktor has sent men from below to see to the upper passage onto the plateau. And do not forget to adjust the light switches. The lights everywhere are to be left on. The Earthquaker does not transmit again tonight. *Verstehen Sie?* Rudi when he returns can attend to Lanz. That young man is going no-where just now. *Schnell!*"

There was the dim thud of heavy boots running, and then only an unintelligible murmur. Professor Bird eased himself from the cot and moved quietly to the door. Pfnür sat at the desk in the shallow alcove opposite, conferring over a chart of some sort with a heavy-set man in a white technician's coat. With a brisk nod, he rose. "Very good, Richter. See to having them crated as soon as Karl and

Rudi return. You will take their post here until then. I must join my wife below and see to our other arrangements."

"Clear, but not All Clear," whispered Professor Bird, sitting on the edge of the cot. "You'd better stay under. We have a watchdog. That is, stay under if you're there at all, and not a vanished pigment." He took the small hand that reached out from under the blanket and squeezed it. "I wonder what that crack about Lanz meant. It's been two hours since they took him out of here 'to ask a few questions.' "

Mab wriggled sideways and lifted the trailing blanket. "He's outside," she whispered. "Somebody swacked him across the side of his head. It looked awful. We—"

"That must have been what I heard just after the first alarm. He must have tried to . . ." Professor Bird's thought trailed off. "*We? We* who?"

"Well—Perry and Hansl Strumpf and me."

There was a long silence. "What in the name of all that's holy—" the professor began. "No. No, I don't need to ask. I take it that your mother is at the bottom of this. How did she get wind of Riensenmoos? And what in blazes was she thinking about to let you . . . What *are* you doing here?"

Mab took a deep breath.

Twenty minutes later the white-coated Richter was still at his post. Professor Bird paced jerkily up and down the short length of the dark cell. "If we get out of this," he whispered drily, "your mother is going to be six shades of green with envy. Molly, cut off from adventure by an avalanche!" He paused, frowning. "Cut off—Good Lord, she won't be! Not Molly. When she comes back from Vienna, no amount of snow is going to keep her out of the Eiswinkel. She'll find herself a guide and come across the shoulder of the pass. Tomorrow morning, probably. She might make it into Pfarr-Werfen tonight, but she'd still have to wait until morning. When she finds you children gone, she'll raise holy hell." He began to pace again, his long legs covering the length of the room in three strides. He shook his head angrily. "Pfnür will have thought of that by now. If he waylays her, or if Hansl and your brother get themselves caught—or you—I won't have any choice. I'll have to do as he asks."

Sitting on the edge of the cot, Professor Bird explained. "Gus Bachner and I had been doing a bit of poking around up on the plateau with no luck. We didn't know what we were looking for. In fact, we'd just about decided the whole thing was a wild goose chase and that the Eiswinkel's being dead center in a pattern of catastrophes was only one of Mother Nature's obscure jokes. But then—the afternoon of the third, I think it was—we got caught in quite a blow up on top and stumbled into a nightmare. The snow was blowing like feathers in a pillow fight when we heard a loud rumble and a high metallic sort of shriek. Then a dim icicle-shape rose up out of a snowdrift and kept right on going until it was as tall as a good-size tree. It was a broadcast tower, but I didn't catch onto that until later. We just stood there, gaping, and missed seeing the characters in the Ice Giant outfits until they were on top of us. Gus broke away in the confusion, but I wasn't lucky." He grimaced. "From the minute Pfnür found out who his guards had bagged, he's been after me to provide information that would increase the efficiency of their blasted Earthquaker."

" 'Earthquaker?' Is that what they call it? Ugh! It sounds like a huge, lumpy ogre who goes around stomping his feet." Mab ran a thoughtful finger along the wire webbing of the underside of the cot. "Daddy? About his wanting you to work for them? I think maybe it's too *late*. I mean, he can't keep us here and all this stuff secret until next winter."

"Next winter?" Professor Bird asked blankly.

Mab explained about the offerings and Carnival and the end of winter and its disturbances. "So after Tuesday it gets shut off anyhow. What is it Doktor Pfnür wants you to do?"

"He wants to know just what cities are in what geologically sensitive areas, and to program his Earthquaker more efficiently, he needs to know some pretty technical stuff about which intensity of tremor would merely shake a certain place up, and how much it would take to inflict real damage. That sort of thing. I had made a pretty good guess as to what was going on with the 'flood insurance,' but this Seismological Forecasting—was that what you called it?—that's a new and smoother wrinkle. Just plausible enough. We may actually have earthquake control and modification techniques worked out in another five or ten years. Oh, there's no doubt Pfnür's clever! He's mad, of course. They're both mad."

Mab shivered. She shifted uncomfortably. "You mean they're doing all this for *fun?*" The stone floor was very hard under her hipbone.

"No." Her father's voice was grim. "Not that they don't

enjoy it, but 'fun' is the wrong word for the exhilaration power can give. And that sense of power needs continual feeding. I think this project must have started out as nothing more than a new twist to high-stakes extortion. The Pfnürs may have meant to salt away a modest fortune in a Swiss bank account and retire to a life of ease. I don't know. But it's clear their appetites began to grow with success. I think you and Perry pieced it out pretty well. The only piece that's missing is how they focus the thing." He sighed. "It's too bad you didn't have a chance to tell your mother about the map. With something like that to go on, she could make a rumpus in the right places and bring the authorities in to investigate."

"Oriole knows," Mab offered tentatively.

Professor Bird sighed again. Oriole never made rumpuses.

Silence closed in like the cramped darkness. Mab's right leg was asleep, and she could not shift her weight enough to help. She wriggled unhappily. Almost half an hour had passed since Perry and Hansl had taken flight. If they weren't caught by now, they must be safe in the snug storage hole despite the four searchers and their powerful lights. "Daddy?" she whispered. "You don't suppose the boys found another way out, do you?"

Professor Bird drew his breath in sharply. "I thought you said you had agreed on a hiding place. If those two young idiots try an unmarked passage, they'll be asking for broken necks—or worse. They could lose themselves for good, deep in the mountain. You'd better hope they *don't* try to find a way out." With a note of encouragement that was almost convincing, he added, "I hardly think they'd try anything that would take them very far from where they lost you."

"Or from the Earthquaker," Mab said, a little sourly. "Scared or no, Perry'd want to see that even if it was going strong enough to shake all his teeth out."

"I suppose so." Her father answered abstractedly, as if he listened for something. A moment later, moving quietly as a cat, he was up and peering through the opening in the door.

"Well, I'll be damned," he said aloud, in slow admiration. "Here indeed's a puzzle stretched upon our curious floor."

Mab was out from under the cot like a shot and limping toward the door as quickly as a heavy, prickled leg would take her. When her father began talking like that—like a character in an old play—he was in a high good humor, and that, in the present circumstances, was a puzzle in itself. He put a warning hand across her mouth and gently drew her in front of him to lift her up so that she could see.

The guard station—table, chair, and Richter—was directly opposite, at a distance of about forty feet, in a shallow alcove. The chair stood squarely beside the table, but Richter—no longer wearing his white coat—lay stretched out neatly on the floor.

"Your young friend Lanz's work, unless I'm mistaken. A very quiet, professional job," he said thoughtfully. Then, remembering caution, he tapped Mab on the shoulder. "Come along, peanut. Down and under with you."

"But, if it was Gabriel, why didn't he let you out?" Mab protested, obeying reluctantly. "Two's better than one."

"That depends on what he has in mind. But he couldn't very well let us out without a key, and Karl is the only one beside Pfnür I've seen with a key—" He stopped, listening. "Someone coming. Are you under?"

146

All Mab in her hiding place could hear was a confused jumble of voices. Professor Bird could make out only a little more: four voices, speaking very rapidly and all at once; footsteps running in the direction of the control room; and silence as someone—Rudi, he thought—tried to ring through to the Pfnürschule cellars. The recollection of the warm, comfortable sitting room that served as the Pfnürs' office— the professor had been taken there the first afternoon— made the dark little cell seem suddenly colder, and he shivered a little.

"No answer." Rudi's voice sharpened nervously. "Herr Doktor Pfnür will be on his way here. Richter must be wakened. Slap him. If that does not work, get some water. What? Well, get them out of the way, dunderhead! They can be seen to later." There was the sound of the telephone button clicking angrily. "*Allo! Kontrol Raum? Allo?* Why in Hades is there no answer?"

Doktor Pfnür appeared at that point, for the voices rose angrily, his among them, and faded off in the direction of the control room. A shadow moved in front of the door as the voices grew indistinct. Professor Bird could not be sure, but he thought he heard, faintly, the high-pitched singing *whirr* of machinery that always preceded the Earth-quaker's transmissions. Yet there was no deadening *thrumm* from the generators . . .

The light that flashed in at the door found the professor to all appearances deep in sleep. "*Er schlaft.*" A deep voice laughed unpleasantly. "Come, stir yourself, Herr Professor. You have company." Keys jingled on a ring, and with a rattling at the lock and a click, the heavy door groaned open. "*Achtung!* In with you!"

A brief scuffle, an indignant but muffled protest, and the

"company" was propelled into the dark room. The door slammed, and the key turned in the lock. "Lanz?" whispered the professor. He knew even before the answer came that it was not Lanz. The company, invisible in the darkness, picked itself up from the floor with a shuffling of four feet and a sullen, waiting silence.

"I believe this is what is called a touching family re-union," Professor Bird said drily. "How did you get yourselves caught?"

"*Pop!* But what—Oh, man, if you knew how *worried* . . . Mom said she knew you were O.K., but Orry . . . Oh, *man!*" Perry threw his arms around his father in an alarmingly strong bear hug.

"Unh! It feels as if you've grown in the last six weeks," Professor Bird said ruefully, as he detached himself. "You'd better come down to earth before Pfnür gets here. Not that I'm not glad to see you." He ruffled Perry's hair affectionately. "But I am *not* glad to see you here and now. Or you, young Strumpf."

The brusque tone was a little puzzling. Perry unzipped his jacket and groped for the flashlight, which he had wisely hidden when the guards began to haul the crates from the mouth of the boys' hiding place. The guards, thinking it a prime joke that their much-feared intruders should be two boys out on a lark, had not searched them.

The light showed a tall, lanky figure, unmistakably his father, despite the six-weeks growth of gingery beard and an odd glint in the usually humorous blue eyes. "Anyhow, you're O.K.," Perry said, somewhat subdued. He sat down beside Hansl on the second cot. "Man, how *wild!*"

Hansl eyed Professor Bird doubtfully. "You do not seem much surprised to see us, Herr Professor."

"That's right. How . . . ?" Perry paused unhappily. It was not going to be easy to admit that he had mislaid his little sister in exceedingly dangerous circumstances. Clearing his throat, he managed a nervous "They haven't already caught Mab, have they?" Hastily, he added in self-defense, "I know we shouldn't have come up here on our own, but we did, and it was partly Mabbit's idea, so we couldn't exactly count her out. I mean . . . well, *have* they caught her? We got sort of separated."

"No need to sound so dismal. They haven't caught her —yet." Professor Bird's voice dropped warningly. "If you'll point that light toward the floor and then switch it off, we'll be considerably safer. We don't want our friend Rudi coming in to take it from you."

Perry obediently dipped the light, and there, just before the beam snapped off, was Mab, grinning out from under the drape of the grimy blanket. "None other," she whispered dramatically, enjoying the boys' astonishment. "They seek me here, they seek me there—"

"Button it up, peanut," was her father's dry comment. "Pfnür may come roaring back here any minute."

Perry sputtered. "B-but you said she wasn't—"

"She wasn't caught, no. You might say I pulled her in through the keyhole. What matters is that they don't know she's here. That may not exactly be an ace in the hole, but any card in a storm, as they say." The professor took up his pacing again. "Your friend Gabriel, now: he's our real hope. He snagged Richter's lab coat, which must mean something. And the control room wasn't answering the phone."

"Perhaps he has went to—how do you say? sabotage the works," offered Hansl.

"It could be, but only as a diversion, I think. Mab tells

me they should be closing up for the season after tomorrow—tonight's was probably the last transmission. Lanz wouldn't think putting the equipment out of commission was worth the risk. No, my bet is that he means to get out as fast as he can. If he makes it, he'll have to convince the authorities somehow to get that road cleared and get in here in a hurry." He sat down and thought for a moment. "If we wait until the middle of the night, we may be able to get Mabbit out without being seen by the man on guard. It's usually Karl, and he sleeps most of the time. With luck she might, just *might* get out the way you think Lanz came in. After that, I don't know. I wish there were some way to get word to Molly," he mused. "The authorities might doubt Lanz, but even if they doubted your mother, they would find it hard to ignore her. If . . ."

"It's no good." Perry shook his head. "No way. Hansl heard one of those men say Mrs. Pfnür was sending up a couple of extra men so they could run double guard all night in that guardroom where the passages come together."

"Do you think they know somebody's still loose?" whispered Mab.

"I do not see that they could," was Hansl's slow answer. "But perhaps they think others know we have come and may be searching for us."

"That's probably it," the professor agreed. "Well. Next idea?"

No one had one.

The voice that speared into the darkness a few minutes later was Pfnür's, but it was a Pfnür without the veneer of civilized charm and regretful concern. The voice was a high, taut, sibilant monotone, a thin stream of acid forced out under great pressure. What it said was quite ordinary, but that made it all the more alarming. "Very early tomorrow morning, Professor Bird," announced Doktor Pfnür, "you will be brought down to the Hochgebirgsschule, where you will be able to bathe and shave and make a change of clothing. Your bags, which we abstracted from Haus Strumpf at the beginning of your stay with us, will be waiting for you. I suggest that you choose a business suit. We have also your overcoat. Your passport will be restored to you at the appropriate time."

"Very kind of you." Professor Bird kept his voice expressionless, but he was wary and deeply alarmed. "When will that be, if I may ask?"

"At the Italian border. We are making a brief stop-over in Italy to gather supplies and to wait for the equipment trucks to catch us up."

"And the boys? I take it that the boys are to remain here." The professor's voice was deceptively soft.

"My young friend Peregrine will come with us, I think. However, I have no need of young Strumpf. He will stay. But you may assure yourself that he will be as if he were in his own bed." There was a touch of mockery in the remark.

"I suppose I must take your word for that," Professor Bird said, but it was clear that he did not. "You might as well leave us all behind, though. I'll be damned if I'll lift a finger to help your crack-brained scheme, now or ever."

"You play with words," Doktor Pfnür snapped. "You will not play with your son's life. There is nothing to discuss. I have urgent matters to attend to. This move has been planned for months; it is only advanced some weeks by the inconvenience of Lanz's escape."

"So he did get away." Professor Bird grinned madden-

151

ingly. Behind him the boys pummeled each other in their relief. "How?"

"That need not concern you. Within fifteen minutes the avenue which he discovered will be sealed permanently. I suggest that you try to get what rest you can, despite the heavy equipment we will be moving past your door for the next few hours. We cannot take all of the machinery, of course, as our transportation is limited to three heavy trucks and the five autobuses."

"Five?" Hansl's terror of this new Doktor Pfnür was forgotten. "But how do you have five? I have never seen more than the one. Or the one truck."

Pfnür's arrogance took on a note of satisfaction. "The peasant simpleton is easily deceived, as you see, Herr Professor. Because no more than one mini-bus is *seen* abroad in the valley at any one time, they assume that there is no more than one, and we are able to shuttle in quantities of petrol and fuel oil under their very noses. There have been difficulties, of course. Frau Pfnür is a genius at planning and schedules, but to have Riesenmoos straddling the road has made heavier traffic impossible, and we need all the time more fuel for the generators. Nothing else has kept us from extending the range of the Earthquaker."

The high, tight voice shook with the frightening excitement of the fanatic. "It is isolation that the Earthquaker needs. Mountainous country where there are no prying neighbors; where we need not keep up a charade such as this farce of a training school, where always we must take care that the few genuine students do not see that they are lambs among tigers. There is such a place, with the water power we lack here for our generators, and where the Earthquaker, transmitting at its full range, can make half the world tremble. Yes . . ." The word was drawn out into one, long *s*. "Yes, we shall sail for Surinam within the week."

"Surinam." Professor Bird frowned. "That's on the north coast of South America." He sounded matter-of-fact, but nothing could have been further from the truth. He was profoundly worried. Pfnür would not reveal such vital information unless he felt himself perfectly safe—not even to impress the professor with his genius.

"Just so. And no roads lead to the eyrie I have found. There is no way in except by helicopter. We will sit atop our mountain and face north across the Gulf of Mexico to all of North America." Pfnür laughed softly, as if he already saw Houston and Mobile and Jacksonville in his sights.

"You're insane," said Professor Bird abruptly. Stretching out on the cot, he feigned disinterest. "When young Lanz gets down the mountain, the first thing he'll do is contact the police. He may not understand much of what you're up to here, but he knows I'm being kept against my will. The police will be in here tomorrow the minute the road crews have cleared away your little avalanche."

"Insane? How fortunate it is, then, that I am not also a fool," snapped Doktor Pfnür venomously, rising to the bait. "My men already are clearing away 'my' little avalanche. We will be well on our way before daybreak. Two of my best men have gone after Lanz, but even if he reaches the *Gendarmerie* in Pfarr-Werfen, he must first persuade the police that there is truth in his absurd tale. Even then, it will be hours before Criminal Investigation officers from Salzburg can be here. I wish them welcome. They will find the whole of the Eiswinkel one great avalanche. No Hochgebirgsschule. No Riesenmoos. A few judiciously placed explosive charges, and the fuel oil left in our storerooms will be enough to make even the Königskogel tremble." He paused, savoring the effect of this news. "But enough: our exodus begins. I hear the first of the equipment trolleys, and I must go down to attend to the packing of my wine cellar and my papers. You will excuse me, I am sure."

The silence in the little room was complete.

eleven

Oriole rolled restlessly from her left side onto her back and glared at the ceiling. It never failed. Just as she was on the edge of dozing off, the puffy down comforter slid to the floor. Retrieving it meant getting halfway out from under the thin blankets into the chilly night air, and she did so with a groan, scrabbling with one hand along the carpet until her fingers met the comforter. In desperation she threw the covers off, wound herself up in the comforter, and drew the blankets up again. Having solved the problem, she found herself wide awake.

Counting sheep was no help. Oriole had tried sheep, rabbits, and Rose Parade floats in succession, all to no avail. Perhaps, she thought in disgust as she turned inside her cocoon, perhaps she ought to try counting Byron Fleischackers. *One* Byron was enough to put anyone to sleep in the normal way of things. She groaned and pulled the pillow over her head. Think of Byron going on and on about his discovery. That should do it. About how exciting and important a find he had made, turning up two dingy, closely-written vellum pages tucked in between two *extremely interesting* (that was Byron being mysterious) pages of the parish register for 1472. About how the date and the newly-discovered ending pointed to *Die Eisschemen* as a Missing Link of the Early Germanic Drama. Oriole wriggled sleepily. Byron was sweet, but—but Gabriel Lanz, at least, was not depressingly *earnest*.

Oriole raised her head. Could that be right? Oriole didn't *like* young men who were not earnest. The pillow tilted and slid to the floor as she raised up, and after retrieving it, she propped it against the bed's carved headboard and sat staring into the darkness. It was dreadful that Gabriel was mixed up in her father's disappearance. It wasn't *right*. Handsome villains were, in the general run of things, supposed to be dark and either saturnine or suspiciously smooth. Gabriel was none of these. Perhaps . . . perhaps, Oriole tried to tell herself, Gabriel had been upset at lunchtime because he feared some danger and had hoped all the Birds were safely away. So he claimed, but . . .

"Mmph!" Oriole gave a gentle snort and tugged the comforter up around her shoulders. "Sounds like one of Mab's silly fairy tales." She yawned as her thoughts drifted. *Gabriel had been heading up the valley. Why hadn't he come back?* He hadn't eaten dinner at the Gappenwirt. Or at the Post, according to Herr Glöckner, who had been recruiting men for the next morning's road clearing. And there had been no light in his attic room at the Metzgers' at eleven, when Oriole walked back to Haus Strumpf, leaving Byron deep in consultation with Herr Glöckner about the exact location of each scene of *Die Eisschemen*. Now, the Carnival images from the church tower drifted near, as fleeting

156

as snowflakes, and then away again as Oriole hovered at the edge of a dream. The sooty, long-eared Fool capered past with his black broom, here and gone and back again, the Ice Ghosts at his heels. They left no footprints in the dream-snow. *Only ski-tracks. How curious to be doing the play on skis. It must be difficult for the players. No—there was only one of him. One dark, sooty figure, swooping, wavering, falling* . . .

Oriole jerked bolt upright at the sound of her own voice. She had been falling . . . "No, it was Gabriel falling," she whispered. Her heart pounded as loudly as if she had been running. "Get hold of yourself, Bird," she said sternly. "It was a only a dream. It *was* only a dream." Nevertheless, her feet crept out from under the covers to feel for the furry slippers on the mat beside the bed. Literally before she knew what she was about, Oriole had draped the comforter around her shoulders, opened the window, and climbed over the sill onto the narrow balcony that ran around the 'house' part of Haus Strumpf. "Idiot! C-complete idiot," she chattered, but no amount of sensible mutterings could erase the panicky sense that something was very wrong, and that something had to do with Gabriel Lanz.

The moon hung in a thin web of clouds, but the night was still bright. There was a wind up, and the only sound was its soughing through the dark hedge of trees that climbed beside the snowy Riesenalm to meet the darker forest. The bare slopes above the forest could not be seen from Haus Strumpf, but the ridge and the towering head of the Königskogel loomed as close as if they had been painted on the blue-black sky above the thick, dark fringe of trees.

Oriole backed away from the balcony railing, shivering.

157

"There's not the least reason in the world I should go up there," she whispered. She marveled that such an idea could have entered her head. "In the middle of the night! And because of a dream? You'll be getting as batty as Mama." Still grumbling, she pattered along the balcony to the window of Perry and Mab's room. Pulling it a bit further open, she peered into the shadowed room and saw that they were sleeping soundly. "Lucky you," she breathed.

In her own room, Oriole picked up the little gold travel clock on the bed table. Two o'clock. "I will *not* go haring up the mountain just because I ate too much *Paprika Schnitzel*," she grated. But as she slipped under the covers, her eyes lit on Mrs. Bird's larger suitcase where it stood beside the wardrobe. That ridiculous ouija board! She had come upon it while looking for some aspirin and been furious. Now she burrowed down, thinking, "If only it wasn't so silly. It must be nice to believe a little pointer can spell everything out for you. 'Yeses or Noes Furnished As Required.'" A long minute passed. One eye opened and fastened on the suitcase.

A moment later Oriole was out of bed and angrily pulling on her tights. "The day I need a ouija board to make up my mind . . ." she seethed. "Well, I *won't*." Two pairs of socks, ski trousers, two sweaters, and a jacket later, she was still angry. Neither of the large flashlights was anywhere to be found. Being in no mood for explanations, she decided not to risk looking in the children's room for fear of waking them. The little pocket flash would have to do. Hastily tying her fur hood under her chin, she pocketed a pair of gloves, eased the door open, and tiptoed downstairs in her stocking feet. The ski boots were lined up in the dark entrance hall, and after one wrong guess, she found her own, snapped the buckle clasps shut, and slid open the bolt on the front door.

With the skins on her skis, Oriole made the top of the Riesenalm in under three minutes. Climbing the rail fence at the edge of the wood was awkward with skis on, but considerably faster than unfastening, crossing, and doing up the bindings again. She had intended, once under the eaves of the forest, to strike straight up the slope in hopes of coming out above the treeline by the shortest route, but the grade was too steep. A quick look around with the help of the little flashlight brought a puzzled frown to Oriole's pretty face. The snow along the fence was trampled with huge, stumpy footprints. Snowshoes, she told herself firmly, but she was not sure. A little further along, these led up a shallow gully angling upward through the trees.

After a moment's hesitation, Oriole struck uphill with a long, easy stride, keeping to the fresh snow alongside the strange track. The heavy footprints made her uneasy, even though the icy film crusting them meant that they could not be fresh. The dark wood was full of shadows, and it took all of Oriole's resolution to keep from peering nervously over her shoulder at every shower of snow from a trailing branch and every rustle of wind through the tree-tops.

Coming out onto the bare slope below the Königskogel, Oriole stopped and leaned on her ski sticks, listening. No one, nothing moved. Nothing but the thickening clouds shrouding the moon. A pity, when she was so awake, Oriole thought, that there was nowhere to go but down again; but the sky promised snow, and soon. If it was foolish to be out alone on a wild goose chase over treacherously icy snow, darkness and a fresh snowfall over that patchy ice could make it perilous. Already the high saddle far up the valley, above the Pfnürschule, was hidden by the distant snowfall as completely as if it had been erased.

But Oriole did not move. Only when the first real squall of wind swirled a thin veil of snowflakes around her and died away, did she bend to undo her ski bindings. The forest track was too risky for a down hill run in the dark. Oriole felt a queer disappointment. She had actually begun to feel more exhilarated than idiotic, but there was no sense in freezing to death because of a wild premonition. Her fingers were prying at a snow-crusted clamp when a long, soft *schuss* of a sound made her raise her head. A hundred yards higher, on the shoulder of the Königskogel, a small, dark figure swept out of a cloud of snow and followed the curve of the hill out of sight.

Oriole was fast. "Ready or not, whoever you are," she said between her teeth. "We'll just see what you're up to." With a jump turn around the pivot of one ski stick, she was off uphill, slanting across the slope at a run. The skins provided a traction that, with Oriole's long-legged lope, had her literally skimming up the hill. In a very few minutes she had struck the lone skier's tracks and, stripping off the skins, set off southward in pursuit without the least idea why she should be doing so, and a great many as to why she should not. A mile whisked past, then two, and always the trail she followed held to the high ground, well above the easier traverses any sensible skier would have preferred. Once, as the prints in the snow told, he had fallen, thrown by a snow-masked rock. He had lost a ski stick, and there were signs that he had had trouble picking himself up with the one left to him.

Further along, on the steep traverse that took them out of the Eiswinkel high above the pass and the climbing road, he had wavered and side-slipped dangerously. Oriole, wondering at such reckless speed, took the long curve out into the wider Wengerau valley cautiously. As she passed above the Werfenweng ski lifts, she was surprised to see her quarry a scant quarter of a mile ahead, running down toward a snow-covered roof bulking out of the drifts in the lee of a great hump of rock. "As the man says, 'In for a nickel, in for a dime,' " Oriole thought, a little wildly, as she raced downhill in his tracks. With a sinking feeling, she realized that something was indeed wrong. Far from speeding recklessly, as the tracks had suggested, he seemed to be in some sort of trouble. The trail she had been following was not so much daring as barely held in control.

"Gabriel! Wait! *Wait for me,*" Oriole shrieked. Her last poor tatter of level-headed caution and self-conscious dignity whipped away on the wind. Gabriel, if it was Gabriel, swerved, coming to a ragged stop a short distance from the hut, and turned unsteadily to face his pursuer.

It was then that the snow shower blowing down off the plateau and through the Eiswinkel Pass caught up with them. Skiers, hut, and the sleeping rooftops of Werfenweng disappeared in a flurry of white.

Oriole wiped clean a circle on the grimy window and peered out. "It's not coming down quite so heavily now," she said. The climbers' hut was still bitterly damp and cold, but the candlelight gave it a cheerful glow. Oriole crossed the room and held out to Gabriel a mug of very sweet lukewarm chocolate, which was all that the hut's larder and wood stove could muster. "How are you feeling? There were some bandages in a kit in the cupboard, but not enough to fix your arm properly. It looks pretty awful. What *happened?*"

Still dazed, Gabriel touched the bandage above his temple, and winced. "What happened? I fainted, I think."

"That's the effect I have on men." Oriole thrust the chocolate at him. "You said, 'Oh, it's you,' and keeled over at my feet. I had to fasten your skis together for a sled to get you down here and inside."

"How long was I out?" Gabriel asked thickly. He pushed himself to a sitting position on the cot and took the cup from her.

"Fifteen minutes. Twenty, maybe."

Gabriel groaned and passed a hand across his eyes. "I must get out of here. I cannot explain now. It is too complicated, and there is no time. I must get to the *Gendarmerie* in Pfarr-Werfen."

"Don't be silly," said Oriole firmly. "It's a doctor you have to get to. That's an ugly gash in your arm. Your makeshift tourniquet hadn't held, but I fixed another, and I think the bleeding's stopped. I ought to loosen it a bit now. What were you up to on the montain to do that to it?" The motherly tone slipped a little as she loosened the Bic pen she had used to wind her silk scarf tight around his arm. "It—it wasn't an accident, was it?"

Gabriel drank the milkless chocolate off with a grimace. "The Pfnürs have a—an illegal transmitter in the caves up there," he said briefly. "I went snooping around and had a warmer welcome than I looked for. I came out the hard way when they left the transmission room unguarded— pushed the 'Antenna Up' button and rode the tower right up through the roof." He grinned ruefully and lay back on the cot, a hand over his eyes. "There were steel support brackets set in the rock wall. I thought the one I hit was going to take my arm off."

"You're lucky it didn't," said Oriole grimly. "And that you found where you'd cached your skis." Twisting the pen tight again, she tucked it under the silk, then pulled the edges of the ripped sweater over the too-skimpy bandage and taped them together with elastic tape. "That won't hold as far as Pfarr-Werfen—and neither will you. Is there a doctor in Werfenweng? You could telephone the police from there first thing in the morning. After all, there's nothing so very dreadful about a clandestine radio station, is there?" She paused, remembering Mab's wild theory. A tiny frown puckered her brows. "I mean, if even *Perry* could figure out about the radio transmissions . . . Actually, what I mean is, it *couldn't* have anything to do with earthquakes and avalanches . . . could it?"

Gabriel pushed himself up, the better to stare at her. "*Perry* has figured it out? But how do you know of the Earthquaker? Your father has told you of his idea before he has come to Austria? Because it *is* truly so. He has explained to me how it works. He suspects that an agent of Herr Doktor Pfnür places at the location which is to be affected a—how do you call it?—a miniaturized 'high-sensitivity amplifier.' A thing perhaps no bigger than a matchbox, and—"

It was Oriole's turn to stare. She was as pale as Gabriel himself. "My *father? When* did he tell you this?"

Gabriel's face was a study in dismay. Clasping her hand in his good one, he said, "*Ach*, forgive me, *Liebchen*. My head is such a muddle that I forget you do not know. Your father is the Herr Doktor's guest under the mountain."

Oriole, wide-eyed, faltered, "Is—is he . . ."

"He is well enough for now, but if the Herr Doktor and his people leave the valley, I think they will not leave him behind. That is why it is necessary I must go quickly to the *Gendarmerie*. You had better come too. I do not think they will follow beyond the pass, but it is best to be safe." He rose unsteadily and, with a quirk of an eyebrow, added "You may end up skiing me down Mountain Rescue fashion. My head still swims."

For a young woman recently given to laboring over the smallest decision and drawing up elaborate plans for every contingency, Oriole moved like a small whirlwind, dousing the fire in the stove with a kettleful of water poured in at the top and blowing out the candles on the way to the door. Only outside, as she knelt to fasten the bindings on Gabriel's skis and her own, did she voice a small doubt. "How many policemen are there in Pfarr-Werfen? Even if they believe you, won't they just send a man or two up to investigate? What good will that do?" Straightening, she found Gabriel already gone.

She had her answer at the *Gendarmerie*. With two respectful policemen hovering nearby and elderly Doktor Schaffer fussing over his arm with a local anaesthetic shot, swabs, antibiotic ointments, and much muttering, Gabriel was very much in charge, telephone in hand. The first call, to the Criminal Investigation Department of the Salzburg police *Kommandopost*, was brief. The second was, astonishingly, to the home of the Minister of the Interior in Vienna. From the little Oriole could make out, it concerned helicopters and Alpine paratroops. When at last the telephoning was finished and Doctor Schaffer had taken thirty-five stitches in Gabriel's arm, Oriole asked warily, "What does that mean—what you said to the police and just now—'*Leutnant*' Lanz, and '*Staatspolizei, Sicherheitsbehörden?*' "

Just as warily—though, after thirty-five stitches, it may have been simply wearily—Gabriel answered, "Federal Security Police, I'm afraid." He sounded apologetic, and the blue eyes watched her a little anxiously. The two sleepy policemen, on being informed that army and C.I.D. reinforcements would arrive shortly before six a.m., the earliest that the road crews could leave for the Eiswinkel Pass, showed their guests into a sparely furnished Duty Room where they could rest. The little old doctor, having fashioned a neat sling for Gabriel's arm, proceeded to dress his head with a bandage that would have done admirably for the Injured Hero in one of Mab's fairy tales.

While the little doctor worked, Gabriel made his explanations. "I have been, as you Americans say, 'undercover.' We have been curious about that elusive transmitter from the first time it blacked out radio communication at the airports in Vienna and Innsbruck, and by the end of this last summer, Riesenmoos had turned up in too many departmental reports for us not to be suspicious. The troubles were too general to seem only coincidence: a falloff in tourism, in lumber and wood products coming out of the valley; the milk cows drying up; the steady increase in medical complaints—"

"*Ja, ja.*" Doktor Schaffer nodded. "Much achings of the teeth. And nervous complaints. Some very interesting cases have come down to us from the Eiswinkel, and by no means all women. Very interesting. So general it was, Fräulein, that my colleagues and I have thought it perhaps some element in the diet. But the agricultural inspectors found nothing.

165

Such a mystery! But if you are correct, Lieutenant Lanz, about this so great high-frequency sound and the deeper vibrations, it could explain all." He snapped his case shut.

Gabriel nodded. "There was a similar case in England a few years ago near a secret government installation using underground generators." He caught Oriole's bewildered look and checked himself. "But you are not interested in details. It is your father you worry about, I know. You must not fret. In a few hours we will have him out safely. Before your mother is returned from Vienna, even. You must get some rest before then and promise not to worry."

Oriole nodded dumbly, avoiding his eyes. With an effort she managed a polite good-by to the doctor. Her feelings were in a jumble. Relief that Gabriel had never been mixed up with the Pfnürs had faded with the realization that his interest in the Birds had been only in the line of duty. He had wanted them out of the Eiswinkel simply to keep them from complicating his job. She wished she could sink through the floor. He was very businesslike, very kind. Just as if she were an—an overgrown child. "No, I won't worry," she announced abruptly, in a tone of bright unconcern, and then immediately felt guilty, because she *hadn't* been worried. At least, not about her father. Since sinking through the floor was not practicable, she sat down on an unyielding cot.

Gabriel's understanding look was unfortunate. Oriole, rattled at seeing that "How transparent you are" look on anyone but family, plunged on with an offhand, "This is all *terribly* exciting. Perry and Mab will be perfectly *green* with envy. Especially Mab. She—"

"Mab." Gabriel sat down slowly, looking, if possible, paler than before. His free hand went to the bandage where

166

it crossed his temple, and his puzzled frown deepened as he held out his wrists to stare at the ugly red welts chafed there by the tight-twisted wire.

"What is it?" Her pique forgotten, Oriole watched Gabriel with real alarm.

"*It was Mab.*" Gabriel stared blindly at his wrists, as if he fished for an image drowned deep in a dream. "The wire was so tight that my hands were numb. I could feel the blood pound in my arms, but I could not awaken—not quite."

"Up in the caves? Yes, but what about Mab?" Suddenly frightened, Oriole slipped her hand in his.

Gabriel shook his head. "It is very confused. There were whisperings, and then, I think, small fingers working at the wire to loosen it . . . long hair brushing my face. It smelled like"—he smiled faintly—"like yours."

"It's the baby shampoo," Oriole explained dazedly. "We both use it. But . . . but Mab was sound asleep when I left the house. Perry too. I *saw* them. In their beds, sleeping like logs."

"Or like bolster pillows?" Gabriel was grim. "No. I am afraid that both of them are inside the mountain. Young Strumpf too, if I know anything. And there's not a blessed thing we can do about it."

twelve

Mab did not dare go further. The rumble of voices might have been twenty feet ahead or two hundred. The caves and passages distorted sound so that there was no telling. Besides, creeping quietly in heavy boots down a steady incline was considerably more difficult than the going up had been. The voices meant that at least two men were on duty in the main guardroom, so there was no getting out that way; and the guardroom controlled not only the way out to the gate and the ladder to the upper passage by which Gabriel must have entered, but the way downward to the Pfnürschule cellars. Mab gave a nervous glance behind her, but the dim corridor was as empty as before. The yellow lights stared, unwinking.

Five minutes of painfully cautious inching gained Mab a shallow niche sheltered a little from the passage lights and within earshot of the guards. What she had forgotten was that they would, of course, be speaking German. She had practically painted herself into a corner, and for nothing.

Their German was harsher, more run-together than the Riesenmoosers'. Mab understood the "*Ja, Kaffee, bitte*," followed by the chink of a coffeepot against a cup; but for the rest she had difficulty making out an isolated word here and there. Then, as she steeled herself to go back and report the hopelessness of her errand, one of the voices broke into a deep laugh as the other gasped out something about "*dumm Heinz*." They laughed so hard, in fact—a word or two, and then a delighted guffaw—that Mab could almost understand. Heinz had done something *dumm* with a *Materialwagen* (a supply trolley, Mab guessed), and the heavy wagon had run off the *Lastenaufzug*, whatever that was, and *gefallen* downstairs. If, that is, *unten* did mean "downstairs."

A chair scraped back heavily, and still laughing, the first man moved to the telephone on the wall beside the passage entrance. He turned its handle briskly to ring the bell at the other end, waited a moment, then, suddenly business-like, said, "*Wagner hier. Alles hier ist gut. Ja. Jawohl, Frau Doktor!*" When he had finished reporting in, the briskness disappeared, and it seemed to take him an age to amble back to his coffee cup. It took another for Mab to turn and tip-toe uphill to a point where the voices were only a dim murmur and she could take a deep breath. Stopping where the shadows were deepest, she stooped to take a look at the floor, and tried to puzzle out what it was Heinz's *wagen* had done. The equipment that had rumbled past Professor Bird's door up until the last hour had been taken down to the Hochgebirgsschule *some*how . . . but how? There were no tracks on the floor, and in any case the cumbersome trolleys would run out of control on such a slope, however smooth. The donkey engine Mab had glimpsed through the window in the wooden door had looked like the sort used to pull strings of luggage carts along railroad station platforms. They were meant for running on the level, not pulling loads uphill or braking downhill. It meant that the Earthquaker equipment was off-loaded and sent to the lower level by some other means. But how? And where? Time was too short to waste it in aimless searching. Mab hated to leave her nice, dim patch of corridor, but there was nothing to do but report back to her father. By now, he would be thinking she had somehow made it past the guards.

Mab moved at a quickened pace up the long slope, hurrying, but careful to step lightly for fear of the echoes that could carry for great distances. By keeping a sharp eye ahead and behind, she hoped to see before she was seen, but the shadowy niches and dark openings made her nervous. Anyone concealed there could see as far as the last and next bends in the main passage and had only to wait until she came in reach. The soft echoes of her own footfalls began to sound like the cautious steps of someone following not far behind.

"Lastenaufzug? That's a freight elevator," Professor Bird had exclaimed. "That shaft Pfnür mentioned! They must have found themselves a vertical shaft and put in a freight elevator." He considered. "It *might* be a way out, but then again it might land you right in the middle of the dragon's lair. Hansl had better go along if we can squeeze him out the hatch. It isn't likely they'll miss him before morning, and if you do, by some miracle, find a way out, the village is going to believe him sooner than you, dear. Understand him sooner, too. Yes. Yes, it *might* just work. Here, let's

see what gear you've got in your knapsacks. That's it. Good heavens—my daughter, the pack rat!" But he had approved the rope and been oddly excited by the can of lemonade. "All right. Now here's what you have to do—"

Finding the freight shaft was not difficult. Only one of the small, dark corridors branching off the main passage had the tell-tale wires that meant lights and traffic. The passage widened after a few yards, but at the narrow entrance the walls were scarred with the bright gashes of metal against stone. The darkness was a welcome touch of good luck. The last workmen must have switched the lights out, forgetting Pfnür's earlier order.

The roof of the passage was in some places a scant inch above Hansl's head, and no more than three inches higher than the train of empty trolleys Mab's muffled flashlight picked out ahead of them. These were like huge baggage carts with sides that let down for unloading, and they had been shunted close along the wall so as to allow room for others to pass. The little donkey engine was nowhere to be seen.

As the wide, low corridor curved toward the right, a rush of chill air met Mab and Hansl. "It feels like the outside-of-doors," whispered the boy. "What time is it?"

Mab pulled the sock off the flashlight. "Half past two."

"I do not know. Even if we are near . . ." Hansl shook his head. "There is my father to convince and the whole of the valley to rouse."

But Mab was not listening. Running, Hansl caught up to her a few yards short of the waist-high iron railing that stretched across the breadth of the passage. At its center was a wide gate, and to the right, a squat, heavy motor and a padlocked shed. Period. The beam of the flashlight skimmed over the ceiling and into the blackness beyond the railing in a vain search for the elevator platform or the festoon of cables that should have been there if the car was at the bottom.

"They've . . . they've dismantled it." Mab's face was tragic.

"No, no." Hansl was suddenly intent. "Shine the light down. In front of your feet, down, yes . . . *there!*" The batteries were getting dangerously low and the beam was too weak to reach far, but it was far enough to show two sets of gleaming wide-spaced tracks and a double cable angling downward. "A funicular," he said. "It is not an elevator lift, but a funicular, or something like. There, there is a light at the bottom. Do you see?"

Looking down the slant of his pointing arm, Mab saw, far below, a dull gleam the size of a half dollar. From the steep line of the tracks and the position of the light below, the shaft must have plunged downward at something like a ninety-degree angle, along the raceway of a long-dead river. "A funicular? Is that like those cable cars in Salzburg?" She and Perry had ridden up the steep Monchsberg to the Hohensalzburg castle high above the town. "There were two cars there. The up one passed the down one in the middle. But," she said, suddenly doubtful, "even if we could figure out how to bring one back up, won't it be too noisy? Noisier than an elevator, anyhow."

"Perhaps." Hansl was unbuckling the flap of her knapsack. "I will look below before we try to bring it up. Here, hold this." Handing her the coil of rope, he fashioned a loop at one end to slip around his waist, and then took the coil and made two turns around one of the supports of the iron railing. "If they have laid tracks on such a slope, there

172

must be steps cut for the workmen," he panted, as he let himself down over the ledge.

A moment later his voice floated up to her. "There are two sets of tracks and steps between, but no rail. It is very dangerous, this stair. *Ach!* The light, it is died. The other is in my rucksack. I am coming up." He did so with considerable puffing and scraping of boots against metal and stone, for the under-face of the ledge—a drop of about six feet—had been blasted out to provide housing for the great cogwheels and cable reels.

The strong beam of the second flashlight turned the loading area into a small, gleaming island surrounded by shifting, flickering shadows. It showed the padlock on the shed, where the children thought to find the controls, to be hanging open on its staple. "They have left both cars somewhere in the middle," Hansl said as Mab tugged the door open, revealing a control panel and two long handles set in slots in the flooring, like old-fashioned railway switch controls. "It is strange that they should do such a thing," he mused, still thinking of the two cars hanging in mid-shaft.

But Mab had seen the cut in the heavy electric cable that snaked its way from the shaft to the controls, and the long-handled wire-cutters that had been used and dropped. "No, just nasty-mean," she said slowly. "What do you bet they chained them together down there in the middle just in case somebody knew how to fix the wiring? I guess that leaves their old steps." She returned to the railing to peer down into the blackness.

"I do not know." Hansl was doubtful. "They are little more than toeholds in some places. They were meant, I think, for coming up as the track was laid; not for going down."

"I went rock-climbing in the Sierras once with Daddy and Perry," Mab said stoutly. "I can do it if you can."

"Very well." Hansl shrugged resignedly. "I suppose I must go first, to stop you when you fall. But before we go," he added hastily, catching the glint in Mab's eye, "perhaps we should attend to the lights, since we do not need the power for the lift."

"O.K." Mab was suddenly all efficiency. "Where's the push button for these ones?" From her hoard she brought out the lemonade and pulled off the pop-top.

"Here," came Hansl's answer. "Here also is a crate for standing on."

They caught themselves just in time. Mab was atop the crate, and Hansl was reaching for the switch when the unspoken warning flashed between them. Professor Bird had counted on the lights being on everywhere, as Pfnür had ordered, when he laid his plans for putting them out of commission. To *turn* them on would be to alert the *Kontrol Raum* that someone had entered the freight shaft.

"There's a lamp in that shed," said Mab after a moment's thought. "Maybe they only keep tabs on where there's a whole string. Let's hope so."

The lamp was an old crook-neck desk lamp, fastened to a staple in the wall, and ideal for their purpose. Hansl twisted the bulb out and bent the neck of the lamp so that the socket pointed up, cup fashion. At a sign from Mab, he pushed the switch at the base and backed away. Mab, squinting and holding the lemonade at arm's length, poured a small amount directly into the socket. The answering flash almost made her spill the rest. Next, they turned the switch to "Off," replaced the bulb, and switched on again. Nothing happened.

"It worked!" Mab crowed. "It really worked."

Hansl moved to the railing. "They are off below, too. It has fused everything!"

"Here," said Mab, taking a quick swallow of lemonade. "Help me get rid of the evidence so I can put the can away. Good." While Hansl retrieved the rope and slipped its loop over her shoulders, she cast a dubious eye over the railing. "If I were writing this in a story," she said, "I think I'd give me shoes with suction cups on the bottom. Do I have to go first?"

"It is better if I handle the rope," Hansl said. "You do not climb with a rope in California, I think."

It was when he had made a second loop and swung down after her that the idea, so obvious that it had gone right by both of them, plucked at Hansl in mid-air. As he gained his footing beside Mab, he was laughing softly. "Do not worry," he whispered. "We cannot fall off the steps. We use the rope to go down, *zzzt, zzzt, zzzt!* No, no, do not undo it!"

Mab had pulled the flashlight from her zippered jacket pocket and begun to work awkwardly at the thin nylon knot. "Leave it on?" she asked. "What for?"

"You will see." The thin rope hummed as Hansl pulled all two hundred feet of it free of the railing support, coiling it as it came. Taking the light, he played it along the near track. The rails were raised above the uneven rock surface and supported at six-foot intervals by heavy steel brackets set into the rock. Around one of these, Hansl made a double turn of the rope, passing the coil around the bracket. Leaving a small amount of slack, he drew it behind his waist and over his left shoulder.

"Now, you must go below me as far as the rope will

allow," he directed. "I do not think we will need the light, but you must cover it for if we do." Paying out slack a little at a time, he backed down to the step above Mab's. "Don't stop," he whispered. "I can tell from the rope how fast you go."

"But there's nothing to hold *on* to!" Mab steadied herself with a hand on the step where Hansl stood and switched the muffled flashlight back on. "It's *weird* in the dark. The way the echoes turn upside down in here, down almost feels like up."

With the help of the dim spot of light, she began to get the hang of it after the first ten or twelve yards, and soon was moving steadily downward. Just short of a hundred feet, Hansl's hand met the metal clip that meant that the end of the rope was coming up. At his whispered warning, Mab stooped and felt for the track to her right and, finding it, held tight. Above, Hansl, running his hand along the track, located the nearest support bracket and sat down beside it to pull in the rope. The only sound for the next few moments was the hiss of the loose end as it snaked upward toward the first bracket, and once or twice a small tinkle from the metal clip. When he had close to a hundred feet loosely coiled, Hansl gave a vigorous jerk and the freed end came slithering down through the darkness. Coiling it, he then passed the rope around the second support, left enough slack so that he could stand, and snubbed it tight. "Ready?"

"I guess. Aren't your arms tired? I once saw two climbers rappelling down the face of the Matterhorn, and it looked so *easy*."

"The *Matterhorn?* They were coming down with ropes?" Hansl shivered. "Surely not."

Mab giggled, backing down to bring the rope between them taut. "The Disneyland Matterhorn," she explained. "I guess it helps if you can see where you're going."

"Um." Hansl, as they began once more to move down the shaft, was too busy with the rope to ask what Disneyland was doing with a Matterhorn, so contented himself with shaking his head. California sounded a most strange and exotic place.

They lost track of how many stages the descent took. Somewhere in the middle they passed between the two freight cars—which actually *were* chained together. After a while Mab had been able to manage without the flashlight, and the last few stretches were quite fast—except for the very last. From a slight drop in the draft that whistled up past them, and the blurred, softened echoes of their footsteps, they knew themselves to be near the bottom of the shaft, but just *how* near came as a shock when a light sprang on in the corridor below. The loading platform of the lift was no more than twenty feet below, and the unexpected light licked at Mab's boots. "Move up," she hissed.

A murmur of voices approaching the loading ramp froze the children where they were. Mab's knees trembled from the strain of keeping balance as she tried not to rest her weight on the rope. Hansl's wrists ached fiercely. Ten minutes to three, Mab's watch said. They had left the top only twenty minutes before, though it seemed more like an hour. Feeling a little as if she were house-fly size and unhappily shut up in one of her own oöstructures, she closed her eyes and tried to puzzle out the location of the voices. They seemed to be approaching from the right, but unless she was hopelessly turned around, the Hochgebirgsschule cellars had to be somewhere off to the left.

"Yes, yes. That is taken care of. Cross it off. And I have set the electronic detonator to the frequency of the car telephone. Check that off, too. As you have seen, the men will have the last truck loaded in a few minutes. I must go up very shortly to collect our distinguished passenger."

The smooth, self-satisfied voice was Doktor Pfnür's. Mab could just see both Pfnürs where they had paused in the passage below, their heads together over a clipboard that apparently held a checklist of What To Do Before The Mountain Blows.

"You must be careful," Frau Pfnür warned, her voice clipped and cold. "I do not like the smell of this blackout business. We have emergency power here, but not above. It does no good to replace circuit breakers when they cannot find what the trouble is. If you must go up, take Kurt and a lantern with you. And your pistol."

"*Ach, Liebchen*, always you imagine dangers." Herr Doktor Pfnür spoke indulgently. "Things had been going very well."

"It is good that someone does," his wife snapped. She took the clipboard. "Come, I must see that Max finishes the burning of the papers we cannot take with us."

"Why bother, *Liebchen?* In a few hours they will be safely buried, deep under the mountain."

"Details one does not attend to . . ." Frau Pfnür began, as their voices moved away.

". . . have a way of attending to one instead," finished her husband. "As you say, my dear."

Several minutes later Pfnür returned, carrying a large battery lantern, on his way to the main passage to the upper levels. Keeping to their shadowy perch for a moment, the two children freed themselves from the rope, which Hansl coiled tightly and replaced in Mab's knapsack. Mab, frowning over Hansl's translation of the gist of the Pfnürs' conversation, guessed that they must have been coming from the garages—and the loading of that last truck. Since there were more trucks than the Riesenmoosers knew about, it was possible that they were actually housed in an outer cavern. The forest crowded against the cliffs on both sides of the Hochgebirgsschule, affording thick natural camouflage. "We can't go that way," Mab whispered. "It might be quicker, but there'll be all sorts of drivers and guards out there. Besides, I *know* the way up through the cellars. *If* we can find them."

The passage, inspected nervously from a corner of the loading platform, was empty except for a fork-lift truck parked near the ramp. More brightly lit than the upper levels—by fluorescent ceiling strips—its stone walls, to make things as awkward as possible, gleamed with whitewash. Not a shadow to hide in. And every sound set up crisp echoes. Mab sat down in a back corner of the platform and removed her boots, pantomiming to Hansl that he must do the same. If they had to make a run for it down a brightly-lit bowling alley of a corridor, they had better be quiet about it. Hansl knotted his long laces together, draping the boots around his neck, but Mab's metal spring fasteners proved as inconvenient as only the latest modern conveniences can be. They could not be hooked together, and there was no room for them in either knapsack, so she edged out into the light-washed passage with a boot cradled awkwardly under each arm and ran.

The passage ended in a smooth, concrete wall bearing in

179

large, black letters the legend *Schliessen Sie immer diese Tür:* Always Close this Door. On the wall to the right two small toggle switches were marked *Öffnen* and *Schliessen.* Hansl indicated the one marked *Öffnen.* As he pressed down on it, Mab shut her eyes and nervously hugged her boots. *"Please* don't let it make any noise!"

No bells rang. The great door did not even groan. Opening slowly outward, it revealed on its inner side a great dusty wine rack complete with dusty wine bottles glued convincingly in place. Beyond, real wine racks masked the doorway from the cellars. The wine cellar portion had apparently been constructed to take advantage of the caverns' coolness in summer. To conceal the fact that the caverns were there at all, the Pfnürs had only to install the camouflaged door.

They had also camouflaged the door switches. Mab and Hansl, once inside, could find nothing remotely like a button or switch. While Hansl searched methodically, Mab, more expediently, reached around to press the one marked *Schliessen* on the passage side, ducking in again as the heavy door swung shut on its slow, silent arc.

The wine cellar, dim and full of shadows after the glare of the passage, was lit only by a narrow wash of light through the half-open door of the room Mab had called the Necromancer's Den; but it was light enough to show that all of the real wine was gone—except for the unlabelled bottles in the rack marked *Vin Ordinaire.* "They're really moving out 'lock, stock, and barrel,' " Mab quipped, but the pun was lost on Hansl, who was concerned only to get as close to the arched doorway as possible without stepping into the light. Beyond the iron-bound oak door, Frau Pfnür sat beside the long table, systematically crumpling papers and feeding them to the blaze crackling in the fireplace. There was no sign of the man she had called Max. From the tell-tale wheezy groan that came from the old elevator in the adjoining pantry, Mab guessed he had been sent upstairs. One less to worry about.

Still, the one left to worry about was enough. Getting to the elevator past Frau Pfnür was not about to be easy, and it would take an age for the poor thing to creak back down from the kitchen. What was needed was a distraction: a bottle of *vin ordinaire* dropped by the cavern entrance so that the old witch would come out and Mab could whisk in? Hansl nobly offered to risk being caught. "Already they may look for me. They would not think of you."

"*Hansl!*" The idea struck Mab in mid-protest. *Hansl. Old witch. And that fairytale room full of statues.* If the key was still in the lock . . . It was crazy, but at this point, what wasn't?

"What is funny? Where do you take me?" Hansl held back as she pulled him toward the other side of the cellar, his whisper soft but insistent.

"Just call me Gretel. And *come*."

The key was there, just as it had been last time. Mab drew Hansl in after her and pulled the door of the statuary room to. In a moment the plot was explained and set afoot. Boots on. Knapsacks off, flashlight unmuffled. The beam was still a bright stab of light. Quickly Mab knotted a pair of the new shoelaces together, tying one end around the flashlight, and looping the other around the desperate Valkyrie's outstretched wrist. A brisk tap set it to spinning wildly so that the light glanced over walls and ceiling, showing here a leering satyr, there a terrified nymph. "That's it. Now we open the door wide and get behind it."

From outside, the light looked even better and, as it slowed, more like someone searching. Mab grasped the two dead batteries from the flashlight that had failed, took a deep breath, and hurled them into the room. As she slipped behind the door, they caromed off the statuary, rattled to the floor, and rolled noisily across the flagstones.

"Who is there?" Frau Pfnür stood in the doorway opposite, silhouetted against the glow of firelight. The children heard the sharp intake of breath as she saw the moving light. "Gert? Klaus? *Was ist los?*" Frau Pfnür's voice dropped to a sibilant hiss. Her footsteps tapped across the flagstones. For one awful moment, when the pale, pudgy fingers groped around the edge of the door to feel for the key in the lock, Mab and Hansl stopped breathing altogether. Frau Pfnür only touched the key and withdrew her hand. Two swift steps and she was through the door. With a cold command of, "Come out, or I lock the door and leave you to wait here for the avalanches," she switched on the lights.

"*Now!*"

The children threw themselves against the heavy door. The hinges had been kept well-oiled, for the momentum sent it crashing shut with such a *crack!* that Mab, startled, was almost a hair too late in turning the key.

"Take it out of the lock," Hansl warned. "If we do not, she will push it out and draw it under the door."

As he spoke, the doorknob rattled, and Frau Pfnür shrieked thinly through the keyhole. "Who is there? Let me out at once! *Who is there?*"

Mab could not resist. Leaning down, she breathed through the keyhole, "*Einzig der Wind!*" Straightening with a grin, she pocketed the key. " 'Only the wind that sighs through the trees,'" she whispered. "Only I don't know the German for all of it."

The puzzled silence on the other side of the door did not last long. The door began to boom as if the marble Swan Knight himself were beating on it. "Come away," Hansl urged nervously. "Where do we go? What if the one called Max should return? We must hurry."

In the pantry, Mab hesitated, her finger hovering over the button that would bring the elevator down. "This thing makes so much racket. . . . What if he hears it up there? All he'd have to do would be to wait at the top until we got there."

"What are these for?" asked Hansl, indicating two buttons next to those for the elevator. "*Ach*, this cupboard—it is what they have at the Hotel Gappenwirt, no? A speechless waiter."

"*Dumb* waiter," Mab corrected, scarcely listening. "There, did you hear that?" She pulled at Hansl's arm in a sudden panic. "He opened the elevator door. Now we *can't* go up. And even if we hide, he'll hear her banging in there, and she'll tell him we're here, and where *can* we hide?"

In desperation, Hansl hit Mab on the back as if she were having some sort of choking fit. "Will you please to be quiet?" he hissed, as she choked in earnest. Quickly sliding the two broad shelves from the grooves that supported them in the dumb-waiter cupboard, he propped them upright in it at the back. Mab watched, bewildered at first, as he tucked himself into the shelfless cupboard, knees against his chest, forehead against his knees. A door clanged above, and with a loud grumble, the elevator began its noisy descent. "Hurry!" Hansl urged. He held out his hand. "There is room if you will squeeze yourself very hard. Quickly. I have done this many times with my friend Freddi Willing in the Gappenwirt, where his mother is cook. There, tuck your foot under. It is O.K.?" He reached out awkwardly with his left hand and pushed the upper button in the paneling beside the dumb waiter. With a jerk the cupboard began moving upward, slowly.

"We are not too heavy, I think, or it would not move at all," Hansl whispered, as they lurched up out of the light and into the dark shaft that echoed with the groaning rumble of the elevator.

"I bet you were a lot littler when you rode in one of these the last time," Mab gasped. The cramped space seemed full of boots and elbows. She hugged her knees close and tried to use her chin to rub the one that had taken a smart crack against the top of the cupboard opening as they got under way. As the elevator groaned past them on its downward way, the bubble of laughter that was never far from the surface began to rise again. "Trains that pass in the night!" she wheezed soulfully.

"Hush, now," Hansl warned. Elevator and dumb waiter had slowed together to a full stop. Taking care to make no noise, the children freed themselves from their pretzel-tangle of knees and boots and slipped to the tiled kitchen floor, Mab first. Hansl, retrieving the shelf boards from the back of the cupboard, fitted them into their grooves and shoved them firmly into place. "There. It is best we do not send it down again, but perhaps now they will not puzzle out how we have disappeared."

"This way." Mab beckoned Hansl past the elevator to a wide, cupboard-lined hallway filled with moonlight. At its end a heavy door with a large, oval leaded-glass window looked out on a strip of snowy garden and a steep wooded slope. "Look," Mab breathed. She pointed out a snowdrift where seven or eight pairs of skis stood like a prickly bouquet, then turned the lock, and eased the door open. "I knew there'd still be some there. I saw 'em the other day." Hansl slipped out after her and drew the door shut. The lock snicked fast.

The skis were all too long, of course, and several precious minutes were lost in adjusting the bindings to the smaller boots, but on foot there was little chance of reaching the village in time. They would have to go by the road. Its patches of hard, icy surface could make it as dangerous as a toboggan chute, and they would risk being seen, but time was too short for anything else.

"*Ach!*"

Mab had one binding fastened when Hansl's startled exclamation made her rise and turn. A tall figure, black against the snow, held Hansl firmly by the collar. Mab twisted away, but not quickly enough to evade the fingers that snapped around her wrist.

The low voice had a chill edge to it. "You will not go just yet, please. I think perhaps we will talk first."

thirteen

LAST TO LEAVE THE CAVERN, THE BIG MERCEDES SLIPPED LIKE a dark shadow through the deserted garage and out onto the moon-white road. It ran without lights. The powerful engine whispered down the winding drive to the gates, purred up a short rise, and then, with a velvety murmur, began the descent to Riesenmoos. Professor Bird and Perry sat, silent and stiffly uncomfortable, in the back seat. Their hands were free. If, when they reached the Italian border, any curious customs guard were to peer in at them, nothing would seem out of order. Despite the appearances, however, they might just as well have done up in mummy wrappings. Tough nylon cords had been wound tightly around their elbows and lashed to the eyebolts for the back-seat safety belts. They could move their hands, but not use them. Ragnar, the huge mastiff, sat upright at their feet, his head stooping a little under the car's roof.

It began to snow. Large, thick flakes. Doktor Pfnür switched the windscreen wipers on and then off again, repeating the action every few minutes as the snowflakes grew too thick to see through. Frau Pfnür nervously slapped the nasty little dog whip she carried against the palm of her glove. "Faster!" she hissed. "Why do you not go faster? In fifteen minutes it is five o'clock. To think of it! Half an hour lost breaking down a door because I was fooled by a child's trick. I have made us too late. I know that those who followed the spy, Lanz, say that his tracks did not go into Riesenmoos, but what of Werfenweng? They could block the road there. And what of the brat Strumpf? Even if he has not roused the village, what of the early risers? The baker's window looks out on the Moosweg. He is sure to see us pass." The words spurted out in angry little bursts.

Pfnür's hand left the wheel briefly to pat her knee reassuringly. "Calm yourself, my dear. Why would they bother to block the road? They think we are already trapped, by the avalanche. I have said it before: Lanz will have gone to the authorities in Pfarr-Werfen. He cannot know how far advanced our plans for departure were, and he is even now asleep, having failed to stir the *Gendarmerie* into ringing up the C.I.D. in Salzburg in the middle of the night. No, my pet, it is not we who should worry."

Frau Pfnür's eyes glinted. One pudgy black-gloved hand reached out to caress the speaker of the car telephone—an odd gesture, which Professor Bird, sitting on the right behind her, shrewdly guessed might have something to do with the threat to Riesenmoos. No one had been left behind in the caverns, so Pfnür must have had the explosives rigged so that he could communicate by voice or electronic signal directly with some sort of detonator. A radio-controlled detonator meant that the whole of Riesenmoos, sleeping unaware, was Pfnür's hostage. Even if young Hansl or Gabriel Lanz had managed to have the road blocked, they would be forced to let the car and trucks pass.

"Where are we now?" Frau Pfnür opened her window a crack and set to defogging the clouded windscreen with her gloved hand. The wipers were going full time as the drift of flakes thickened. Suddenly she leaned close to the glass, peering fiercely out into the shifting white blur.

"Where?" Pfnür pulled out a handkerchief and wiped his own side of the windscreen. "The Mooserkreuz, I think. *Ja*, there is the shrine." He looked at her and then back at the road. "Klara? What is it that you see?"

Frau Pfnür's small mouth thinned into a chill smile. "*Einzig der Wind*," she said obscurely, but with an air of deep satisfaction. "You are right. Fortune has not deserted us after all. Turn off the motor, but do not stop. *Quickly*." She wound down the window on her side.

Pfnür switched off the ignition and slipped into neutral gear. The big car floated silently down the gentle slope, and in a moment Perry and his father, straining to see, could make out a small figure limping along the side of the road several yards ahead. Even before the figure turned to peer toward the car looming out of the snowy darkness, Perry knew that it was Hansl. His stomach felt as if it had just taken a long plummet in an express elevator. *Mab. Where was Mab?* He met his father's eyes across the dog, who had shifted and was now sitting between them and resting his chin on the back of the front seat. Professor Bird was equally alarmed, but it was an alarm that was almost immediately replaced by a puzzled frown. Perry

188

was opening his mouth to call out a warning when his father raised his forearm, lowering his head a little to meet it, and laid a finger across his lips. Bewildered, Perry obeyed, and together they watched helplessly as Hansl turned in a confused circle, then plunged up the bank and stumbled toward a break in the fence.

The car stopped with a jerk. Frau Pfnür, straining over the back of her seat, opened the rear door. *"Fangen Sie!"*

The mastiff lunged out of the car over Professor Bird's legs, nearly removing a knee in the process. Four lolloping strides and the huge dog overtook the unsteady Hansl, flattened him with a nudge of the shoulder, and stood grinning with one great paw planted on the boy's chest.

"Good beast." Frau Pfnür puffed up the little bank, her husband close behind. On command the dog returned to the car, clambered back over Professor Bird, turned around on the seat in a tangle of legs, and with a warning glare, settled down as before. The Pfnürs came struggling behind, Hansl draped between them.

"If you've hurt him, you . . ." Perry's angry outburst died as the Pfnürs deposited their burden on the front seat. There was no mistaking it. Hansl's eyes opened, and one drooped shut in what looked incredibly like a wink. A quick glance told Perry that his father had seen it too. His shoulders relaxed a little, but his thoughtful expression did not change. *Mab*, they were both thinking. *Mab must be out too, and safe. For the moment.* By the time Frau Pfnür was seated and Pfnür around at the other door, Hansl had slipped sideways, limp and apparently unconscious.

"Exactly." Frau Pfnür, her good temper (such as it was) restored, gave Perry a placid smirk. "If he is hurt, threats cannot help him." She pulled Hansl up so that Doktor

Pfnür could slide in behind the wheel, and the Mercedes, still without headlights, moved off with a deep, confident purr. Inside, in the comfortable insulated quiet, no one heard the deep, clear belling of the alpenhorn.

The snow came down thickly. It began to blow a little as the Pfnür car moved down into the pass through a Reisenmoos fast asleep except for a dim light glowing at the rear of the church. There was not so much as a glimmer at the bakery. The road below the village was treacherous in spots where the new snow masked ice, but in less than ten minutes the car's occupants sighted the truck drawn up on the left ahead. Or four of the occupants did. Frau Pfnür's pinches and shakings roused Hansl to no more than a restless stirring and moaning.

"He has fallen in the road, perhaps, and hit his head on the ice," she said impatiently. "*Ach,* we have no need to question him anyway. It would be simplest to stop here and roll him over the bank into the Riesenbach, *nicht wahr?*"

"Not now." Doktor Pfnür raised his hand in salute to the driver of the first VW bus as he passed it. "Time enough when we are safely away. There is a nice little precipice just this side of the Plockenpass that will do." He spoke over his shoulder. "My dear Professor Bird, I am afraid it is the degree of your cooperation which will determine whether your son goes that last stretch to the border with Max, cross-country, or, er—remains in Austria with his young friend here. There is the small matter of a passport. I have yours, but there is none for the boy."

Professor Bird made no answer. There was nothing to say. Instead, he kept his mind firmly to the problem of the

Strumpf boy and what he was up to. There had to be a way to sabotage the car telephone, and only Hansl could do it. The difficulty was in letting him know without alerting the Pfnürs.

"Here is Max." Doktor Pfnür braked gently to a stop and rolled down his window as a bulky figure loomed out of a snow flurry. "Maxl!"

"*Herr Doktor!* I had begun to worry." Max leaned on the car door and peered in curiously. "Nothing went wrong, I hope?"

"Nothing that is not repaired. But why is the road not clear? We are running late. Surely you have had time to do as I ordered."

"*Ja, Herr Doktor.*" Max flushed and drew himself to attention. "We have cleared as far as our marker. We stopped four feet short of the point reached yesterday by the emergency crew from Pfarr-Werfen, so that no one can tell from below that we are here. I have the snow plow truck at the head of the line. Follow me, and as soon as I am through the drift I will pull aside to let you pass."

"Very good." Pfnür revved the Mercedes' motor. "Get on with it, then."

The snowfall had dwindled to a few stray flakes. Above the reach of the headlamps and behind, the narrow pass was as dark as if it were still middle-night. The truck at the head of the line, almost invisible in its fresh gray paint and the gray plastic tarpaulin covering its load of heavy equipment, stood a few feet from the white wall across the road, its snow plow raised. As its motor started up with a rumble, Doktor Pfnür left the Mercedes idling and climbed out to watch the plow lowered. Frau Pfnür and the dog Ragnar joined him as it dropped with a screech and a clank. It edged forward, scraping along the rutted ice of the road at an angle, and pared a thick swath from the snow barrier, nudging it over the bank into the Riesenbach gorge. Men moved in with shovels to knock down some of the overhang left by the blade. The truck reversed, then moved up to scrape this fresh fall away as it made a second slice.

"*Hansl?*" Professor Bird kept his voice low. "Can you hear me?" The boy had slid down out of sight on the front seat when Frau Pfnür left the car. Perhaps he actually was faint or dizzy, but it had not looked as if the dog had hurt him. No answer. "Hansl, if you can hear me, don't answer. Just see if you can reach that radio phone." He did not dare speak more loudly. The Pfnürs had left both car doors open and stood together not ten feet away.

"Pop! He's awake, Pop," Perry whispered. Not bound so tightly as his father, Perry had, with some concentrated wriggling, loosed the knots enough to raise himself up in a crouching fashion. By craning, he could peer over the top of the front seat. Sitting back hastily, he tried to mask his excitement. "*He already knows.* Something must be up."

Hansl was not only awake. He was busy. Crouched low on the seat, he was completely invisible from where the Pfnürs stood, but Perry had seen first the thin fingers struggling to open the blade of a small clasp knife, then one hand darting out to feel where the microphone cord emerged below the radio speaker.

"Let's hope that's the only way they have of detonating those charges. I'd hate to be wrong," was Professor Bird's uneasy comment at Perry's excited whisper.

The words dropped into a sudden, unexpected silence. Outside, everything had stopped: the mutter of voices, the clank of the snow plow, the grinding shift of truck gears. Down into that silence fell the ghostly notes of a distant alpenhorn. "What in Hades is going on out there?" Professor Bird scowled, twisting around in an effort to see. And it was worth seeing.

The snow barrier toppled slowly with a rich *phlumph!* As it came down, the Pfnürs came face-to-face across the tumbled heap of snow and ice with two even larger snow-plows equipped with spotlights and bristling with armed soldiers. As the lights sprang alive, so did the narrow curve of road ahead, doors opening all along the line of three police cars, an army troop carrier, an ambulance, and a long, black Cadillac flying two small American flags on its front bumper.

Herr Doktor Pfnür was most impressive: his calm; his genial assumption that the reception committee had nothing to do with him; his gracious insistence that vehicles traveling uphill had the right of way and that he would move the Mercedes immediately to allow the cavalcade to pass. Only when he recognized Gabriel Lanz, arm in sling, as he climbed from the first police car, did he pale. But even then he did not despair of carrying it off. Lanz had not actually seen *him* up in the caverns. He could not have seen enough to understand fully what he had stumbled into. No, a failed climbing trainee with a grudge against the Pfnürschule should not be too difficult to discredit.

"Lanz, my boy! It looks as if you've had another tumble. Nothing serious, I hope?" The Herr Doktor's voice held a nice mixture of concern and joviality.

"No, nothing serious." Gabriel did not look directly at Pfnür, but past his shoulder. What did Lanz see? Doktor

193

Pfnür resisted the qualm that tempted him to turn and see what caused that slight relaxation and kept his eye instead on the impassive Gabriel and the heavy-set, overcoated man who joined him.

"Why, it's Captain Hirsch, isn't it?" Pfnür beamed. "How good to see you again. But what brings the Salzburg C.I.D. into the Eiswinkel at such an unholy hour?" Turning slightly, he said, "Klara, my dear. Move the car in behind Max's truck so that these good people may pass." Frau Pfnür had already edged as far as the open door on the driver's side.

Captain Hirsch looked distinctly uncomfortable. He eyed Gabriel doubtfully as Doktor Pfnür turned back and dropped his voice to ask, "What is all this, Herr Captain? Training maneuvers for the Alpine troops? Or should I ask? Don't tell me they have you running interference for the army with the local population these days. Community relations, eh?" Curiosity seemingly put him in a gossipy mood.

Captain Hirsch grew even more uneasy. He knew nothing but good report of Pfnür and had, in fact, heard him talk at an Alpine Club meeting or two and enjoyed his wit and dedication. A sound man, Captain Hirsch would have said, if a bit odd-looking. Vienna had better know what it was up to when it set its agents onto a respectable citizen like Waldemar Pfnür. Kidnaping, among other things, Lanz had said. The whole story sounded incredible. Clearing his throat, Hirsch said drily, "You'll have to ask Lieutenant Lanz, I'm afraid."

Pfnür's eyebrows went up, politely skeptical. "Lieutenant?"

"*Ja, Leutnant. Staatspolizei, Sicherheitsbeamten.*" Gabriel spoke crisply. "I think we've had enough of this little charade. You and your people are all under arrest."

"Under arrest! By whose orders? On what charge?" Pfnür's shocked amusement increased Captain Hirsch's discomfort.

"By order of the Minister of the Interior, on charges of destruction of public and private property, for a start. International sabotage. Extortion and kidnaping. Enough?" Gabriel bowed ironically. "Now, if you don't mind. I believe Herr Professor Bird and his son are with you. The American Vice-Consul and Professor Bird's wife and daughters are here to meet them." He looked up briefly as a dim clatter passed overhead. "Perhaps I should also tell you that when the order is passed, the helicopters you hear will land men on the plateau, and behind you in the village."

"I see." The words slid out like little snakes. Straightening, his smile chilly, Pfnür took a step backward. "Indeed, I do see. But you do not. You will order the road cleared ahead and allow us to pass. If you do not, every soul in the Eiswinkel, including ourselves, will be buried under fifty feet of snow. If we are not interfered with, I will consider releasing my, er—guests. Klara?" He turned and nodded sharply. When Frau Pfnür, blinking owlishly in the glare of the spotlights, had slipped into the driver's seat, the silkiness left his voice. "I advise you to be quick. There are explosive charges set all along the west rim of the valley, and they are rigged to a tremblor detonator which operates on the frequency of my car telephone. Frau Pfnür has only to say one word, and . . ."

"Waldemar!"

"Do not distress yourself, *gnädige Frau*." Captain Hirsch,

195

convinced at last, was grim. "There *is* no one in the valley. All of Riesenmoos has crossed the Pass by the high trail to Werfenweng. The alpenhorn was their signal."

"Ah, but *you* are here, *Kapitan*," Pfnür hissed. "So it becomes our freedom in exchange for *your* lives."

"*Waldemar!*"

Pfnür turned to see his wife's round face with its little blackcurrant eyes pucker up like a baked apple as she glared at him in balked, bewildered fury. "*Waldemar! Es ist nicht hier!*"

Hansl Strumpf—the source of Gabriel's relief of a few minutes earlier—moved out from the shadow of Max's truck. "Is this what you are looking for?" He held out the speaker of the car's radio-phone. "It will be difficult to repair very quickly, I think."

fourteen

"I'VE FOUND BYRON! HE'S IN HERE." MAB'S HEAD APPEARED in the doorway of the church's tiny muniments room as she called to Perry. Turning back to stare at the litter of typewritten papers strewn along the bookshelves and over the floor, she asked, "Were you here all night? You might've been blown to *bits*."

"This," said Byron, red-eyed and tousled, "is *Die Eis-schemen!*" He beamed in triumph. "The real, complete thing. The mystery of the Ice Ghosts is solved! It took all night, rooting through old records, but everything falls into place." He brandished a handful of papers. "I've got it all: the lost bits about the *Frühlingmädchen*—the Spring Maiden—and what the animal- and flower-headed children did, and why the play was stopped after 1472, and the ending torn out of the play-book—everything. But there isn't time to explain now. You'll see it all this afternoon." He looked at his watch. "Lordy, how did it get to be noon? You two better run along. Father Sepp and I have to go over this new material before the rehearsal. Let's see . . . I *did* the translations into modern German; now, where . . . ? Oh, here we are."

Byron stuffed the sheaf of papers into his attaché case, snapped the catch, and only then looked up. "Blown to bits?" His brow puckered in vague concern as he looked from Perry to Mab. "Did you say something was blown to bits?"

Perry nudged Mab, who would have happily launched into a lurid account of the Whole History of the Affair Pfnür. "It was nothing much," he said, perfectly deadpan. "We can tell you later. But it's nice to know the mystery's solved."

Byron bustled them out ahead of him and turned the great iron key in the lock. "Yes. I knew I'd solve it sooner or later, but the timing couldn't have been better."

"I s'pose not." Mab watched, bemused, as Byron disappeared into the sanctuary in search of Father Sepp. "He really is hopeless," she sighed. "You don't suppose Oriole—"

"She isn't *that* square," Perry said. "Come along. Let's go see if Pop's back from Salzburg yet."

Professor Bird turned up in a rented Volkswagen in time to sweep his family and the Strumpfs off to a festive lunch at the Hotel Gappenwirt before the afternoon's festivities. There was quite as much talking as eating, but the professor managed to put away an impressive lunch in spite of the barrage of questions and Mrs. Bird's free hand tucked in his. The elder Strumpfs shook their heads in bewilderment at the unfolding details of the Pfnürs' grandiose plot. Even Molly stared at news that the police, in tracking down the Pfnürs' Swiss bank account, had found that it already held well over a million dollars.

"But how did they *do* it?" Perry leaned across the remains of his paprika chicken. "I know about the Earthquaker's transmitter, but how did they work it at the other end? You just can't focus radio waves on a small enough spot like some sort of—of sound laser."

"I don't know about that. But what they did was actually very simple." His father rescued an untouched crispy roll from Oriole's bread plate just as the waitress was about to remove it. "Frau Pfnür, you see, turns out to have been an electronics genius. The whole plot dates from the day about five years ago when she succeeded in miniaturizing an ultra-high-sensitivity receiver-amplifier. Weatherproofing and all, she got it down to a very thin, flat disc no bigger around than a bicycle reflector. The transistor micro-circuits could have fit on a chip about the size of Mabbit's little fingernail."

"So small as that!" Herr Strumpf shook his head. "Such a device could never be seen in the snow. And it would not be difficult to take them past the *Zoll*—the customs."

"Right. Every time Pfnür left on one of his lecture tours, he had a supply of the things taped under a false bottom in his attaché case. The police think he must have disguised himself and used hired cars for the actual planting of the devices. At least, no one answering his description seems to have been seen near any of the disaster sites. It was all very well plotted."

"Frighteningly so." Mrs. Bird rummaged in her shoulder bag. "Here, I forgot all about Skinny's cablegram. It came through this morning right after the telephone lines were repaired. He says Seismological Forecasting, Inc., really does live out in Antelope Valley. It consists of one secretary and a duplicating machine, and the girl claims she never knew the source of the bulletins she mailed out." The cable was passed to Professor Bird. "I wonder if that wasn't the flaw in it all. Their being *so* very devious and clever, I mean. If you think you're being terribly clever, at some point you must begin to think everyone else pathetically stupid. It was all very well to fake a message from Gus Bachner's doctor to lure me out to Vienna, but apparently it never occurred to them that the children weren't some sort of helpless luggage I just happened to have along."

Frau Strumpf, who had pecked at her lunch like a small, dazed bird, ventured a timid question. "Herr Professor Bachner, he is in the *Krankenhaus* yet?"

Molly nodded, "*Ja, aber* he really is much *besser,*" falling back into her habit of using whatever German words she happened to remember. "After *ich sprach mit* him, I took *ein Taxi* straight to the Embassy and made a dreadful scene. In self-defense the Ambassador finally got in touch *mit der* Minister of the Interior, but *they* wouldn't move until they'd heard from Gabriel Lanz."

Frau Strumpf, having understood little more than the "yes" and the "better," nodded with interest but, during the following pause for the arrival and cutting of a handsome chocolate cake, leaned toward Hansl for a whispered translation.

"What about all that Surinam stuff?" Perry watched his plate as it made its way around the table. "Was that really true?"

Mrs. Bird, Oriole, and the Strumpfs had not heard about Surinam. "I thought he was raving when he came to that,"

Professor Bird admitted. "But they had not only bought up a big tract of mountain wilderness there, but three French cargo helicopters to go with it. There actually was a freighter on the way to meet us at Mestre, the port on the mainland near Venice. Mad. Absolutely mad." He shook his head wonderingly and, like the others, turned his attention to the generous slice of *Sachertorte*.

Later, over coffee, Herr Strumpf chuckled contentedly. "*Ach*, do you know, I love best of all the tale of shutting up the old witch. I never have liked that woman!" Catching Hansl's delighted grin, he recovered some of his usual gravity. "All the same, you were very *glücklich*—very lucky—not to be caught."

Mab, who had been temporarily silenced by an ill-judged second helping of cake, rolled her eyes. "Me, I nearly *died* when I thought we'd been caught. To come all that way and get stopped outside the back door! And then it was only Ferdi Friml."

"Ferdie?" Oriole roused a little from her moody isolation. "His name's *Ferdie?*"

"Well, 'Ferdinand!' "

"Poor thing! But how come he believed the two of you? It must have seemed an incredibly batty story."

Hansl, with helpful interruptions from Mab, explained that young Herr Friml shared a room with two other climbing students who, similarly, suspected nothing of the goings-on inside the mountain. As the weeks passed they had grown uncomfortable at the Pfnürschule, but it was nothing you could put your finger on: just a vague uneasiness. Last night at nine o'clock, however, Frau Doktor Pfnür had appeared at their door with a pot of hot chocolate and a smile meant to be motherly. As soon as the

dragon was gone, Herr Friml, who did not care for chocolate, split his mug between his friends. When not five
minutes later they were deep asleep and snoring, he was
perhaps a little surprised; but it was when the sound of
engines wakened him in the small hours of the morning,
and he found the door locked fast and could not stir his
friends, that he had become alarmed. Remembering the
removable bar on the window—an exit developed by an
earlier occupant—the indignant Herr Friml had tied his
bedding into a makeshift rope and slid out into the night
to investigate.

"The big garage doors were open, and he'd seen the
trucks loading," said Mab. "That's why he believed us.
And when Hansl went down along the road, so's to catch
the Pfnürs when they came out, Ferdi took me to see Herr
Musser, the woodcutter. He belongs to the local Mountain
Rescue Service." She grinned. "Ferdi told him Herr Doktor Pfnür had said to spread the word that a fire had
started up in the caves, and there were a lot of old World
War II explosives stored up there, so the whole valley
ought to be evacuated."

"Did he, now?" Professor Bird laughed. "A very clever
young man, your Ferdinand Friml. With a story like that,
no one would stop to ask questions. We ought to recom-
mend Herr Friml to the Federal Security Police, don't
you think?"

"Where *is* Gabriel?" Oriole asked quietly, putting down
her coffee cup.

"Still in Vienna, I expect," was her father's offhanded
reply. "They flew the Pfnürs there within half an hour of
our arrival in Salzburg."

"Then if we leave first thing tomorrow morning, we won't see him again." Oriole sighed philosophically and then quirked a rueful smile at Mab. "So much for all your plots!"

"Who, me?" A flustered Mab swallowed the last of her cake.

Molly Bird eyed her elder daughter with interest. So direct an Oriole was something new. It would take some thinking about. Meanwhile, there was the quirk to her husband's eyebrows, and before his curiosity could lead to a tactless question, she raised her own in warning. Turning to Frau Strumpf, she said hastily, "It's almost three o'clock, and in all the excitement we've forgotten the Carnival play. When does the procession start? Er . . . *Wenn beginnt der Faschingsspiele?*"

The Riesenmoosers began taking up places along the Moosweg before five o'clock. Rumor had it that the young American, Herr Fleischacker, insisted that the players' procession reach the center of the village just at dusk. No one knew the reason for the change. Father Sepp merely beamed and talked obscurely about Restoration, and the Wisdom to be found in Pagan Symbolism.

At the Gappenwirt, Professor and Mrs. Bird and Oriole (looking very pretty in braids and a Riesenmoos costume) held places of honor next to the Mayor on the front balcony, overlooking the Moosweg where it widened into a tiny square. The Mayor, who had very little mayoring to do except on such special occasions, turned out to be the children's old friend Herr Glöckner. Perry and Mab he sent off to follow the procession in from the Mooserkreuz.

"*Ach*, you must not miss the Fools," he exclaimed. "When the procession comes to the churchyard is soon enough to join us here."

A small crowd, some of them strangers to the village, was gathered across the road between the Mooserkreuz shrine and the Pension Mooserkreuz, where the garage, formerly the barn, had been decorated with jagged, icicle-slats to suggest the yawning mouth of an ice cave. Byron Fleischacker, a head taller than most of the crowd, was not hard to find. Hailing Perry and Mab, he volunteered his services as translator and offered Mab a boost onto a nearby stone wall. Though not tall enough to see, she was clearly too grown-up to scramble through the thicket of legs.

Eventually, after several earnest conferences with a tall shadow lurking inside the icicled door, the orchestra—an accordion, two violins, and a drum—struck up a solemn fanfare to announce the Ice Ghosts' approach.

"Well, what *do* you know!" exclaimed Byron. "That's from *The Magic Flute!*" However, any description of Mozart's opera was forestalled by the appearance of the first Ice Ghost, nine feet tall and only a little less alarming in the daylight than his Pfnürschule step-brothers had been by moonlight. Behind him came two more, and behind them another two, the five together drawing the sixth and most awful in a high-prowed, oddly boat-shaped sleigh. Its high back was like a square sail, and the white "boat" had been sprayed repeatedly with water until it gleamed with ice.

Raising a hand that held a wavy-bladed wooden sword, the sixth Ice Ghost announced,

Ich bin der alte Eiskönig,
Und heute ich werde sein
Von Moos der König endlich,
Und immer Winter werde haben.

"He says," whispered Byron, "that he's the old Ice King; that at last he's going to be king of Moos, and we'll have winter forever. 'Moos' was the old name for Riesenmoos."

The little crowd drew back to watch the swaying Ice Ghosts form a circle in the snowy road and perform a ponderous little sword dance that ended with the destruction of a harvest display of apples, corn, and hay set up near the roadside shrine. Then the procession began, demons, empty ice-boat, band, and silent onlookers marching along to the doleful drum; but at the next house along the road, the tension shattered. At the Ice Ghosts' drumming on a shed door, a raffish, red-nosed old man tottered out, waving a sharpening strap in one hand and a pot in the other, to pause unsteadily and bow. "*Ich t-tritt herein als Rastelbinder,*" he announced with unsteady dignity. Then, donning the pot as if it were a crown, he hiccupped his way through a verse Byron's whispered translation gave as:

"*I am the master tinker.*
In Moos there is no faster drinker.
I mend pans and I drain pots,
And you may call me King of Sots."

Cutting a wobbly caper, the tinker peered foggily at the demon beckoning him along and—to the cheers of friends in the audience—led the way to the next house. Here the drumming on the door brought out a marvelously ugly old crone, apparently a favorite of the crowd. "*Ich tritt herein als die Klatschbase,*" she cackled, dropping a mocking curtsey.

> "*A slanderous gossip I may be,*
> *But what's a nasty name to me?*
> *The ones I fashion for my neighbors*
> *Give my tongue its sweetest labors.*"

Twirling a noisy wooden clacker, Gossip hobbled to join Tinker in discovering the ice-boat, and for the next few yards, they rode in style. Their antics and cheerful insults aimed at members of the crowd made people forget the menace of the wintry demons who drew the sleigh along. At the third stop, they collected a dim-witted butcher, brandishing a heavy whetstone and blustering, "Pigs, chickens, calves, geese—What be they but meat, bones, grease?" After the violent butcher came a fat and prosperous gentleman, who wore a large key on a chain around his neck and rubbed his hands greedily as he confessed that,

> "*I am the Mayor and baker of Moos.*
> *Ach, I stuff myself like a goose!*
> *Krapfen or Strudel or Topfen cake,*
> *I eat the first batch of whatever I bake.*"

But the last was the favorite of the smallest children. A delighted voice at the front of the crowd piped "*Der Faschingsnarr!*" as the booming on the fifth door died down, and, far above, a sooty face crowned with donkey's ears popped up from the chimney. A moment later the long-legged chimney-sweep had tumbled down the roof into a deep drift. The others pulled him out, and the *Narrenschiff*—the "ship of fools"—set sail for the village center, three of the Ice Ghosts drawing it, and the passengers pelting each other with snowballs all the way. Looking after them, the towering *Eiskönig* raised his sword to his two companions triumphantly and trumpeted, "*Ich bin der Eiskönig . . .*"

> "*. . . and these my fools.*
> *Who welcome old winter and laugh at rules.*
> *They think tonight they'll rule all Moos!*
> *The fools! They've only set us loose!*

Byron boosted Mab up onto the churchyard wall. "Here's where it all starts to come together," he whispered. "The fools always go in to pull the harvest display to bits—because the demons can't cross onto holy ground—but this time they have an added attraction among the vegetables."

The clowns and the audience along the wall discovered her at the same time: a green-gowned girl in a corn-colored cloak, wearing long blond braids, a corn-husk ruff, and a crown of ivy. She perched among the apples and potatoes like an outsize corn-husk doll. The crazy dance that reeled along the churchyard paths seemed beneath her notice, and the Ice Ghosts outside her caring, but not so she to them. The forces of ancient myth and the passions of the old play stirred in the watchers as the edge of the music sharpened, and the giant *Eisschemen* swayed before the church gate, calling softly to the Maiden in desire and hatred:

> "*Mädchen, Mädchen,*
> *Winteres Liebchen—*"

Old Gossip, quick to see where advantage lay, slipped from the dance. There were whisperings at the gate, and then there passed between the *Eiskönig* and the Gossip a ball of ice that, marvelously, became a fat and rosy apple as the old crone held it up. "*Ne, ne,*" murmured some in the crowd. "Oh, no!" Mab echoed. "It isn't that, is it?" But Byron was busy frowning at a pushy stranger with a camera.

The apple was a beauty—Appleness itself—and the Maiden smiled to see it. But each time she offered it, canny Gossip drew back quickly, as if she dared not touch her foot to the church steps. Yet surely such an apple should crown the heap of fruits that were a thanksgiving for the harvest past and a reminder of earth's promise? The Maiden stepped down. Once swept into the dance, she laughed to see the apple bob always a step ahead; and because she watched only it, in a twinkling she found herself outside the church gate and the apple in the palm of the Ice King's hand.

In the same moment that she smiled and took it, the Ice Ghosts surrounded her like a chill cloud across the sun and swathed her in a snowdrift of a white sheepskin cloak. They swept her with them into the little marketplace, and the Fools of Moos came clamoring after. The Fools of Moos indeed: for now the Tinker lost his pot-crown, Gossip her clacker, and the surly Butcher his precious long whetstone. The Sweep was swept into the *Narrenschiff* with his own broom, and the dumpling Mayor wept at the loss of his key to Moos. There was no music in the deepening dusk; only the wailing of the Fools cowering in the ice-boat, and the clash and stamp of the winter demons' triumphant sword dance.

"Once upon a time," as Byron put it, there had been a well in the center of the marketplace—crowned, perhaps, like other town wells in Austria, with a handsome wrought-iron canopy—but all that now remained was the base of the stone well-head. In the summer, flowers grew in the carved stone basin covering the forgotten well, but now a large, round mirror lay on the snowy surface, representing the water beneath. Here the Ice Ghosts brought the unsuspecting Maiden and stood her on the step.

Once it must have been more truly frightening: to see the demons clearly in the magic water, to see the crown of ivy gone, and prickly spruce set in its place; pot and whetstone now crown and scepter on a dreadful king; and darkness falling to the tune of harsh laughter and a clown's clacker.

> "*Heil Eiskönig,*
> *König im Moos!*"

The poor maiden, all despairing, bit into the apple. No one, Mab learned afterward, had ever known why. Perhaps because it looked alive when nothing else was. What mattered was that the apple was a lie. The maiden fell across the cold stone ledge, one green arm trailing in the mirror-water.

> "*Heil Eiskönig,*
> *König im Moos!*"

Dusk was darkening into evening. Suddenly, like sunshine spearing through dark clouds, torches sprang up upon the hillside and bells gave tongue along the paths and alleys on the hill—brassy handbells, the *tink-clank* of cows, and a silvery clatter like a company of goats. "*Raus, raus, raus von Moos!*" The chant came first from the strange torch-bearing runners converging on the square and in a moment was taken up by the crowd. *"Out, out!"*

Wheeling away from the well, the Ice Ghosts drew together in a tight ring, facing outward against the threat of light and sound. The Fools cowered in the ice-boat. The demons' swords wavered in the gathering torchlight, and the watching crowd gasped in recognition. The gleaming faces below those flickering lights were dream-images from an all-but-forgotten past: cow-eyes and velvet noses, sheep's eyes and curling horns, sunflowers and white-petaled, brown-faced daisies. Antlers flickered in the shadows. Crowns of grape leaves gleamed, and cornsilk manes shimmered as light and warmth and wood and field streamed into the tiny Marktplatz. *"Die Kinder im Riesenmooserwerke,"* someone breathed. The carved "Riesenmoos work" figures were come to life.

"Raus, raus, raus von Moos!" cried the running children. And Winter broke. Its demons fled the warmth and light and mocking bells, breaking through the crowd, taking to the Moosweg, to passageways and crooked alleys. The running children snatched up the traces of the ice-boat, and the Fools were whirled away, willy-nilly. The villagers, first a few and then all, took up the chant of *"Raus!"* and joined the laughter and the chase. It was over in no time, though *"Raus!"* and laughter and the jingle of bells sounded on the outskirts of the village long after the Ice Ghosts had fled and the Fools were reported "melted and sunk as they sailed down the Riesenbach."

Mab was fretting about the poor Maiden, abandoned at the well, when the animal and flower children reappeared to lead the way back to the marketplace. But not light or bells or the little band's valiant attempt at a melody called *"Frühlingstraum"*—"The Dream of Spring"—could rouse her. As the churchbell began to toll, it looked as if the music from "Death and the Maiden" would have been more appropriate. *Six. Seven.* The great bell in the church tower was not ringing six o'clock on a cold February evening in 1972, but that deep midnight which could be either the edge of every springtime yet to come or be the End of Things. *Eight.* The cows lowed, and the flowers drooped . . . and the band almost missed its cue. *Ta-ta-ra, ta-ta-ra!* sang the accordion, hoping to be taken for a distant trumpet. *Ta-RA!*

Mab, back on her perch atop the churchyard wall, clung to an ironwork gate support and craned to see, for up the Moosweg from the lower end of the village, mounted on Herr Glöckner's Gretel, a knight came riding. If his plated armor (Fräulein Muhlbach's triumph in *papier-mâché* and silver paper) was more appropriate to an emperor than a knight, it was because the only medieval armor pictured in the school's history books happened to be the Emperor Maximilian's. A bloodied bandage bound the hand that held his lance, and he rode wearily into the expectant silence. *Nine.* To the wood-children and field-children who came to hold his bridle he gravely said,

> *I met six giants on the road*
> *Who would not let me pass.*
> *I raised my shield and drew my sword,*
> *And shattered them like glass.*

Ten.
Dismounting among the gathered torches, the knight signed that he was thirsty, and a score of eager hands drew him to the well and the Maiden. *Eleven.*
Mab shut her eyes.

"Well, I couldn't help it. I couldn't *stand* it." Mab stumped along, trying to stir the circulation in her frozen toes. All around, people were embracing, laughing, or singing *Mein schön Moos* with sentimental gusto. Lights had sprung up along the crooked street, and men were homing in on the *Weinstuben* of the two hotels while wives and mothers hurried home to put the finishing touches on this last feast before Lent. "I mean, I knew what was going to happen, so I didn't *miss* anything," Mab said defensively. "He *had* to kiss her, and she had to wake up and see his reflection over her shoulder in the well, and they go off to live happily ever after and all that. It—it's just that it made me go all cold and—*squishy*. I guess . . ."

"*I* guess you're tired. Who isn't, after last night?" Perry changed the subject hastily. He was certainly too tired to listen to Mab vaguely *squish*ing. "Did you see old Byron zoom off after the guy with the camera? Somebody said the magic words '*Time-Life*' and he was off like a shot."

"Honestly? Where?" Her alarm at the power of fairy-tales-in-the-flesh forgotten, Mab brightened. "Do you suppose he *will* get to be famous?"

"Could be, I guess. But I'll bet they came because somebody heard about the Earthquaker, not an old Carnival play." Perry grabbed Mab's elbow. "Hey, look! There's Gabriel. Getting out of the blue VW." But before the children could thread their way among the cheerful groups of Riesenmoosers, Gabriel and the driver of the blue *Polizei* VW had disappeared through the Gappenwirt's front door.

"Quick, up the outside steps!" hissed Mab, suddenly not in the least tired. She ran for the stairway at the rear of the little hotel's side balcony.

Above, the rest of the family and Herr Glöckner were sitting on the carved railing, listening to an excited Byron's report that *Life* was taking him to dinner for an interview about "this Carnival Week excitement."

"Wait'll they hear *his* version," Mab whispered mischievously to Perry before they rounded the corner.

"Oh, old Byron's all right. At least he ought to get a good dinner out of them. Go *on*."

"What I don't understand," Oriole was saying, "is why the play was ever abandoned—in 1472, you said? There's nothing dreadful in it except the Ghosts, and they *kept* them. I thought it was wonderful."

"Ah!" Byron was back in his element. "It was what wasn't *supposed* to be in the play that did it. Once upon a time—1471, to be exact—after the Ice Ghosts were routed, the knight and the earth-children came back to find their poor old Spring-Maiden had fallen down the well. By the time they got her out and home, she was quite an icicle. There must have been a lot of superstitious muttering, because the parish register of deaths says, 'All pray God's grace it be accident or human act.' But it was the next year that really did it: the Maiden disappeared altogether, and the scare was on. My theory is that she eloped with a traveling minstrel—someone from Outside, at any rate—and picked the one time and place when no one would be thinking of such a simple explanation, and so no one would raise a hue and cry after them."

Herr Glöckner chuckled. "You are right, I am sure of it! Perhaps with the Ice Brides it was the same. It is a nice thought."

"I've had a nice thought of my own," said Professor Bird abruptly, his eye caught by a movement in the upstairs hallway. "Now that we know Riesenmoos so well, it would be nice to think that we might come back before long. Say, next year, for winter sports?"

"Daddy!" Oriole, whose back happened to be to the door into the hall, lit up like a Christmas tree. "It—it *would* be a lot more fun than Aspen," she hedged, recovering.

"One condition." Professor Bird's eyes met his wife's. "*If* all three of them will learn—really learn—some German by then."

Oriole's glow faded. "But I have a full schedule these next three quarters." She considered. "I know Mab and Perry can go to Mrs. Strauss after school or on Saturdays, but she doesn't tutor in the summer. I suppose I could take it at PCC . . ."

"Yes, there's that," said Molly, bending her All-Seeing Gypsy look on Professor Bird. "But I think your father may have something else in mind—"

The professor grinned. "What your father has in mind, Ariel, is the six-weeks' summer course at the University of Vienna—if you can earn something toward the airfare between now and then. Unless, of course, you prefer Pasadena City College." He stood, ignoring her blank surprise. "Come along, Molly old girl. No need to stay out in the cold forever. Herr Glöckner, Mr. Fleischacker? Will you join us in a pitcher of *Glühwein* over at the Post and some dinner? Good! Molly, you lead the way."

A thoroughly bemused Oriole turned to see Byron steered firmly by the elbow toward the corner leading to the outer stair. Only then did she catch sight of the open door into the hotel's upper hallway where Gabriel stood, his eyes tired, but laughing. "The Pfnürs are safely tucked in," he said, "so I thought I'd better get back before the Birds flew away."

"Come on," hissed Perry, as Mab hung back. "*Come on!*" He gave her arm a sharp tug, and together they slithered around the icy corner, crack-the-whip style. "I thought this was the bit where you shut your eyes, anyhow." He laughed, propelling her firmly toward the stairway.

"Not when it's *Orry*," protested Mab. "Besides, it must not be that. He was *laughing* at her. And *Orry* was laughing. So it *couldn't* be that. Happy endings are always— well, fairy tales are *serious*."

"So is laughing," countered Perry, with a wisdom beyond his usual. Pleased with the thought, he nudged Mab down another step and decided he wasn't too tired for dinner after all.

They found Byron stopped on the bottom stair, where he turned in slow puzzlement. "What on earth did that fellow mean by that crack about the Pfnürs? Where *were* they all day?"

Mab and Perry looked at each other solemnly.

"Well, you see," they said in unison, taking a deep breath and settling down on the snowy steps.

"Once upon a time—"